PRAISE FOR IRIS MORLAND

## PETAL PLUCKER

Funny, charming, and utterly captivating! I devoured this sparkling read.

— ANNIKA MARTIN, NEW YORK TIMES BESTSELLING AUTHOR

Petal Plucker was funny, entertaining, fresh and fan-yourself-worthy . . . Their enemies-to-lovers romance is both charming, tender and steamy, and you'll love both of these characters (and their families!) and their sigh-worthy happily ever after.

— MARY DUBÉ, CONTEMPORARILY EVER AFTER

Morland has created a masterpiece of a romance . . . one of my favorite [books] of the year.

— CRISTIINA READS

Humorous, raunchy, and refreshing, Petal Plucker has rightfully earned its way, in my opinion, as one of the best romantic comedy [books] this year.

— CAROL, TIL THE LAST PAGE

## My One and Only

This book was gripping, well written & the chemistry between the characters sizzled throughout this wonderful read.

— AMAZON REVIEW

## All I Want Is You

Another heartfelt, steamy, terrific story. This is an author who really knows how to create a story that catches a reader's attention and characters that capture her heart.

— BOOKADDICT

### Taking a Chance on Love

Thea and Anthony are in for a surprise when it comes to the language of the heart . . . I am in awe.

— HOPELESS ROMANTIC BLOG

## Then Came You

This story really pulled all my heartstrings. This was truly a beautiful story and makes you believe there really is true love out there.

— MEME CHANELL BOOK CORNER

# ALSO BY IRIS MORLAND

## ROMANTIC COMEDIES

He Loves Me, He Loves Me Not

Petal Plucker

War of the roses

## LOVE EVERLASTING

*including*

## THE YOUNGERS

Then Came You

Taking a Chance on Love

All I Want Is You

My One and Only

## THE THORNTONS

The Nearness of You

The Very Thought of You

If I Can't Have You

Dream a Little Dream of Me

Someone to Watch Over Me

Till There Was You

I'll Be Home for Christmas

HERON'S LANDING

Seduce Me Sweetly

Tempt Me Tenderly

Desire Me Dearly

Adore Me Ardently

# SOMEONE TO WATCH OVER ME

## THE THORNTONS

## IRIS MORLAND

BLUE VIOLET PRESS LLC

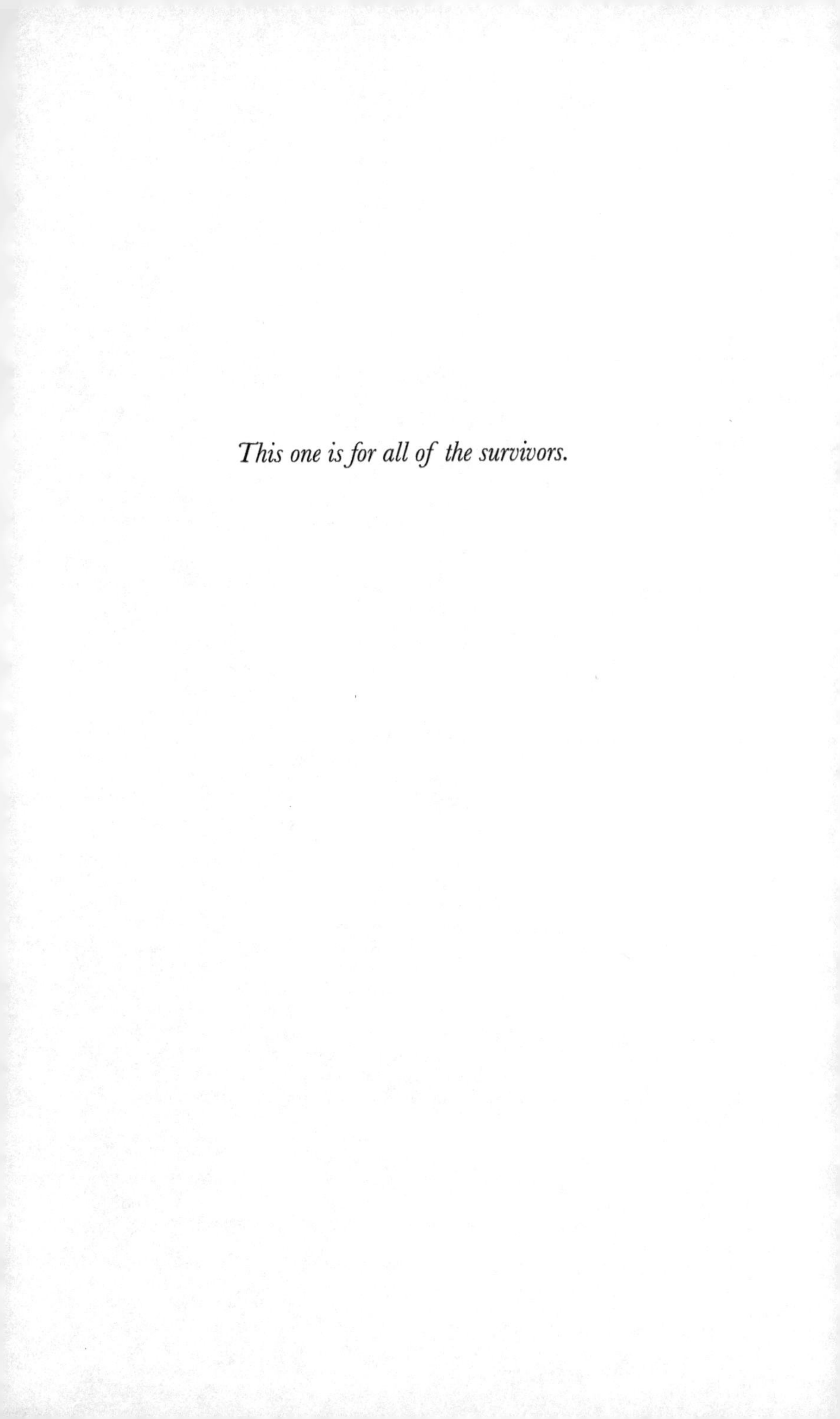

*This one is for all of the survivors.*

# SOMEONE TO WATCH OVER ME

# CHAPTER ONE

**B**lood, sand, heat. It smells of copper and he can't see anything in front of him. He shouts, hoping he's not the only survivor, and he hears a groan through all of the noise. He wonders if his eardrum is blown from the blast.

He follows the noise. It's instinctual at this point. He wonders if he imagined it when he can't find the source of the sound. Then: he sees something. He kneels next to his comrade, gently turning him over. He doesn't know if his friend is dead. When he hears him choke and gasp, he realizes he's alive.

But given the wound in his belly, he will be dead within minutes.

He tries to get his friend up, get him help. He can't die out here when they're going home in a week. Not like this. His friend has a new baby girl and his wife needs him—

Another blast rocks him. He collapses onto the sand, hits his head on something hard and painful, and it all goes black.

SETH THORNTON barely caught the scream in his throat as he woke up. Thrashing under the too-heavy bedcovers, he sat up, gasping for breath. He could taste the sand and blood on his tongue, even though he'd been in Fair Haven, Washington, for a year now. After his third tour as a Marine, he'd finally earned inactive duty.

Except that inactive duty had meant that Seth had no idea what to do with his life now. Who was he, if not a soldier? He knew war; he knew guns; he knew death and he knew victory. But mostly, he knew loneliness, and it was like a pall he couldn't overcome. Even with his twin sister, Lizzie, getting married and having a baby, even knowing he could do whatever he wanted with his life now, it wasn't enough.

He blew out a breath. "I'm turning into a total sap," he muttered as he got up. After taking a quick shower and getting dressed, he made himself a cup of black coffee—his usual breakfast—and after he'd downed the mug, he decided to get some fresh air.

It was better than sitting in that apartment and reminiscing about his best friend's death.

Outside, it was an obnoxiously beautiful day. June in Washington State heralded the end of the rainy season, and the sun shone so cheerily that Seth scowled up at the sky. What did the sun have to be so fucking happy about?

It didn't help that he had nightmares more often than not. When he could sleep, the memories crept up on him, taking over his dreams, until he'd wake up even more exhausted than when he'd gone to sleep. Lizzie had stopped asking about the dark circles under his eyes because he tended to snap at her, but he saw the worry in his twin sister's expression

*You can't keep going on like this,* she'd said just a week prior. *Nobody can.*

He would, because he didn't have a choice.

Right then, Seth heard a woman swearing. Very colorfully, in fact. Intrigued, he rounded the corner to see an overstuffed armchair seemingly hanging in midair, the only evidence of human involvement being the slender ankles and feet standing on the concrete. The woman swore again as the chair began to tip onto the ground.

Seth grabbed the chair just in time. It was heavier than it looked. Grunting, he was about to ask which apartment the woman lived in when he was arrested by a face that he couldn't forget.

Rose DiMarco. The woman he'd met outside The Fainting Goat, the most popular bar in town. Those wide blue eyes, that pert little nose. The dark brown hair tipped with blue.

She stared at him in surprise. "You."

"You," he drawled. "How have you been, princess?"

That pert little nose wrinkled. She tried to lift the chair away from his hold, but he had at least a foot on her and a whole lot more muscle.

"How about you tell me which apartment is yours, unless you want to stand out here all day?"

Rose hesitated before sighing. "It's number 115. Just right around the corner here."

Seth's eyebrows shot up, but he bit his tongue in time. It just so happened he lived in number 117—right next door.

What a fascinating coincidence.

They maneuvered around the corner and into the apartment, setting the chair down with a thud in the mostly bare living room. Seth took in the boxes—most labeled BOOKS—and then he took in Rose herself.

Her long hair was in a braid down her back, her cheeks flushed. He told himself she was flushed from the exertion, not from him, but it amused him that she not only remembered him, but that she'd reacted to his presence so decidedly.

He'd seen her outside The Fainting Goat fending off some asshole, and when said asshole had grabbed her, Seth had come to her rescue. Except that Rose had taken issue with his interference, and Seth had wondered where the hell this beautiful, fiery woman had come from. He hadn't seen her in a month, no matter how many times he went to The Fainting Goat. He'd almost wondered if he'd dreamed her.

Now here she was. His new neighbor.

A smile tipped up his lips, and when she saw it, she put her hands on her hips.

"Thank you for your help," she said in a prissy voice, "but that was my biggest piece of furniture."

"So you're saying I should leave?" Now he was definitely amused.

"Not in so many words."

"Are you always this kind to people who help you?"

She opened her mouth and closed it, looking very much like she'd like to stick out her tongue at him. Instead, she decided to turn around and say nothing.

Seth followed her to a hatchback outside. He wondered how she'd gotten that chair in her car in the first place. He saw boxes and more boxes, along with random odds and ends: pillows, blankets, picture frames. Except that the picture frames held no pictures in them, and her pillows and blankets and lamps and everything else were as nondescript as Rose was colorful.

He picked up two boxes, and when she looked like she'd balk, he just raised an eyebrow.

By the time he'd helped her get everything out of her car, her apartment looked slightly less depressing. He noticed she had no bed to speak of. Would she sleep on the chair? On her floor?

He suddenly wanted to know everything about her. What kind of a woman carts five boxes of books and no bed to a new apartment? No pictures, no knickknacks. He hadn't seen boxes labeled clothes or shoes or jewelry like his sister Lizzie had had when she'd moved in.

"Is there a moving van coming?" he asked, intrigued.

Rose looked up from the box she'd begun to unpack. "A van? No. This is it."

"Are you getting a bed later today?"

She wouldn't look at him as she began to stack books. "No, I'm not."

Well, that said plenty. But at her warning look, he decided not to push his luck. He started to help her unpack her books, glancing at the spines as they started to shelve them in a tiny bookshelf that wouldn't hold even half of her collection.

Jane Austen, Charlotte Brontë, Elizabeth Gaskell, John Keats, Shakespeare, Virginia Woolf, Charles Dickens—so many books, most of which had clearly been read over and over again. Some were falling apart, barely glued together. When he took out a copy of *Frankenstein*, the cover fell off entirely.

"Oh, poor guy. This one has been through a lot." Rose took the book from him, smiling.

That smile burst something inside him. Something hot, something dangerous. Something that felt exactly like *longing*. He caught his breath and forced himself to look away before he got burned.

After they'd shelved as many books as they could, Rose stood up, wiping her hands on her shorts. "Do you want something to drink?"

She didn't wait for his reply. She returned with two glasses of water and handed one to Seth, which he took gratefully. And he realized, with an inward start, that helping Rose DiMarco move in had made him forget this morning's nightmare.

At the thought of her last name, something itched in the back of his mind. He knew that name, didn't he? He looked at her more closely, trying to find a clue, but all he saw were those bright blue eyes, like the lake on a sunny day. He'd never seen eyes like hers. As he gazed at her, he watched as a blush climbed up her cheeks.

So she wasn't as indifferent toward him as she pretended to be. That only heightened his attraction. His blood thrummed.

But then something fearful flickered in her eyes, and she looked away. He recognized that look all too well: he'd seen it in the eyes of his men when they were facing down death. He'd seen it in his own face.

But what did Rose have to be afraid of?

Rose DiMarco, in all of her twenty-seven years, had never encountered a man as *stubborn* as Seth Thornton.

Yes, this was the second time she'd met him. No, she didn't really know him. Yes, she had thought about him more often than she cared to admit after he'd saved her from Rich, one of her ex-boyfriend Johnny Porter's cronies.

She'd moved to Fair Haven to escape—and to escape from men who wanted to use her for their own gains and pleasure.

She recognized desire in men's gazes. She was no stranger to those heated looks, those looks of anticipation. It was rather like having a large predator spot you and decide to hunt you down. Running only made them want to hunt you more.

Rose had no intention of being the gazelle to Seth's lion.

*He looks more like a panther*, she thought as she looked at him out of the corner of her eye. *All muscle and darkness. And those blue-green eyes. Like turquoise.*

A dog barked from her bedroom. Rose jumped, feeling foolish. She'd left her German shepherd, Callie, in her bedroom while she'd been moving in, forgetting her when Seth Thornton had appeared. Guilt assailed her as she went to let Callie out of her tiny bedroom.

Callie was all black, and small for a German shepherd. Rose had gotten her from the shelter three years ago, and Callie had proven herself a worthy companion and guard ever since. Rose had needed a large dog to keep people at bay; Callie had fit the bill perfectly, even though she was more likely to demand belly rubs than take a bite out of some villain.

Callie woofed, her tail wagging. She followed Rose into the living room, going alert when she scented Seth. She sniffed him. Rose couldn't help but notice that Seth allowed the dog to smell him without moving. Most people tended to reach for dogs without considering the consequences.

"This is Callie," Rose said.

Seth waited another moment until Callie had completed a thorough sniffing. Deciding that Seth wasn't a threat, she sat on her haunches, watching him with her dark eyes. Sometimes Rose wondered how much Callie perceived in people.

Seth kneeled down, and when Callie wagged her tail, he began to stroke her silky dark head. Callie woofed in pleasure, her tail wagging harder. A smile spread across his face.

"Pretty dog," he murmured. He gave her one last pat before rising. "Is that it?"

"Is what it?"

His smile widened. "Is that everything you needed out of your car?"

"Oh!" Rose barely stifled a blush. "Yes, thank you. You don't need to stay." She winced and, feeling foolish, decided to focus on unpacking the few things she had.

But what could she do with blankets and pillows without a mattress? She hadn't lied when she'd said she didn't have a mattress being delivered anytime soon. Her brother, Heath, had said he'd buy her whatever she needed, but she'd declined. She'd taken care of herself for this long; she didn't need anyone's charity. Although, if she thought about how she could barely afford this apartment, she knew her pride would only last so long. She had agreed to borrow his car for the move, but that had been the extent of the charity she'd been willing to accept.

She tossed a blanket, annoyed with herself, and she heard Seth grunt a laugh.

"What did that blanket do to you, princess?"

She almost growled. "Will you stop calling me that?" She

moved past him to go into the kitchen to get…something. More water? *Maybe I'll just hide in a cabinet until he finally leaves.*

Callie sensed her sudden tension and pressed her wet nose against her palm. Rose stroked along Callie's spine absent-mindedly.

"Are you stalking me?" she blurted. At his raised eyebrow, she added, "Because isn't it kind of weird that you keep showing up to help me? What do you want from me anyway?"

His lips twitched. "It's a small town."

"It's not that small."

"True. I haven't seen you in a month. Usually people run into each other more often than that."

*That's because I've been avoiding you.* She'd seen him at The Fainting Goat, where she worked as a waitress. Every time she'd seen him at a booth or at the bar, she'd somehow sneaked into the back or persuaded a coworker to get his order.

She hated people helping her. Treating her like a princess. Princesses were kept in towers, hidden away, waiting to be rescued. Rose refused to wait to be rescued, because she knew all too well you'd be waiting for the rest of your life.

"Were you looking for me?" She wanted to sound accusatory; instead, she sounded breathy.

"I wanted to know if you'd gotten rid of your stalker. Did you?" His eyes darkened ever so slightly. "Did that asshole leave you alone?"

"For now."

When he looked like he wanted to ask more questions, she shook her head. "I still don't get why you're at my apartment complex at all." A frisson of fear coursed through her. Had her instincts been wrong again? Was Seth no different from Johnny?

Ice coated her veins at the mere thought.

But Seth only laughed. "Nothing like that." He pointed over his shoulder. "I'm in 117."

"Wait. You live here?"

"Generally more than one person lives in an apartment complex, yes."

"You're my neighbor."

"So it would seem."

She blushed scarlet, and then when he stepped closer to her, she blushed even redder.

"I think you're the one stalking me," he said in a low voice that made her blood simmer. "Although I can't say that I dislike the idea."

She wondered if he would kiss her. She wondered if this was what it felt like to be a gazelle when a lion spotted you. Yet the question begged to be asked—did she want to be caught this time?

She swallowed. She couldn't tear her gaze away from his. With his height, his dark brown hair, his chiseled jaw, and those bulging arms, she would have to be deaf and blind not to notice how attractive he was. A faint beard darkened his face, although he probably had a five-o'clock shadow every evening despite shaving in the morning. She couldn't help but notice the cleft in his chin, and the way his upper lip curved. All of him seemed hard, unyielding. Ruthless. A white scar cut along his left cheek, and he had smaller scars on his arms and his hands.

Callie barked, the moment shattered. Rose jumped away

and tugged at her braid. She felt dizzy. She wished Seth would leave so she could find her equilibrium again.

"Let me take you out for drinks," Seth said suddenly.

She almost laughed. She hadn't gone out for drinks—gone on a date—in years. An eternity. Rose wasn't the dating type. That was for women who didn't wake up terrified of the memories, the past, the ghosts who would never let her go. Dating was for women who weren't scared of every man they encountered.

Dating was for women who didn't see danger around every corner.

"I can't. I'm busy." It was a lame excuse, but it was all she could come up with. Normally she could tell guys no more smoothly, but Seth was something else entirely.

She expected annoyance, but Seth just said, "One drink, then. It's not marriage. You don't even have to pay for it."

That made her laugh. "I hope not. Isn't the guy always supposed to pay?"

"Now you're being archaic."

She laughed, and when his eyes crinkled, her heart did that annoying little flutter in her chest. It was on the tip of her tongue to say yes when her front door opened.

"Rose, hey, I thought you'd like some coffee," her brother, Heath, said. When he saw Seth Thornton standing in her living room, he stopped in his tracks.

The trio all stared at each other. Rose suddenly felt like she'd been caught doing something naughty, and based on Heath's irritated expression, she'd have to explain that nothing had happened.

*If only my brother wouldn't treat me like a child.*

Seth's eyes widened. Then: "You're his sister."

"Yes. Did you not realize that?" She was confused now.

Seth shook his head. "DiMarco. Of course. I should've known."

Heath pressed one of the cups of coffee into her hand before asking in a deceptively casual tone, "So, how do you two know each other?"

CHAPTER TWO

S eth considered Heath DiMarco, whose expression looked
very much like he'd enjoy throwing Seth out on his ass.
Seth had known that Rose's last name had rung a bell, but
he'd been so wrapped up in *her* that he'd never considered that
she had an older brother.

An older brother who was currently bristling with protective instincts.

Heath was shorter than Seth, but Seth had a feeling the
elementary school teacher had more to him than he let on.
Despite his glasses and his quiet demeanor, something lurked
beneath that calm façade. Seth had encountered too many
men trying to hide their darkest parts not to recognize it now.

Seth had met Heath a handful of times when Heath had
joined the Thornton brothers for drinks. Heath had been a
good friend, especially to Harrison, and to Harrison's wife,
Sara, when she'd begun teaching at Fair Haven Elementary.
Seth knew little about Heath, though, and since he'd been
gone from Fair Haven for so long, he was at a loss at how to
respond to Heath's automatic antipathy toward him.

"Have you two met?" Rose said brightly—too brightly. "Heath, this is Seth Thornton. Oh, you must be Harrison's brother," she said, almost to herself.

Seth smiled grimly. "I have three brothers, actually. And two sisters."

"Too many damn Thorntons around here," Heath muttered.

Seth saw Rose register surprise; he had a feeling her normally quiet older brother was never this irritable around company.

Heath finally held out his hand, which Seth shook. Heath's grip was clearly a warning, and Seth only gripped the man's hand harder in response.

*Be pissy if you want. Your sister is a grown-ass woman,* he thought.

Of course, he could admit he'd acted similarly when Trent Younger had come sniffing around Lizzie last year after he'd broken her heart. Seth hadn't minced words with her ex—who was now her husband and the father of her child—and Seth and Trent had only come to an understanding after punching the shit out of each other.

"You live around here?" Heath inquired.

"As a matter of fact, I live next door. Funny, right?"

"What a coincidence." Heath turned his attention toward his sister. "What all do you need help with? Sorry I couldn't come earlier."

Seth knew when he'd been dismissed. Giving Rose a salute, he left, knowing full well that Heath DiMarco was staring holes into his back.

Seth collapsed onto his couch and drummed his fingers against the cushion. Seeing Heath act like some protective

Neanderthal over his sister should've given Seth a very good reason to leave her be.

Yet he felt the opposite—it made him want her all the more.

What was it about her? For some reason, she reminded him of a hummingbird: all fluttery and colorful, flitting from flower to flower. Delicate and small, yet able to weather more storms than you'd expect.

He rolled his eyes at himself. Soon he'd be writing poetry about her. A hummingbird, really?

Next he'd be buying her flowers, taking her to fancy restaurants. He rubbed his temples at the thought of what came *after* going out to dinner.

Would she blush that same shade as he undressed her? He realized with a groan that her blush was probably the same color as her nipples.

Seth had enjoyed beautiful women before, although since he'd been on three tours, he'd never had time for a real relationship. When he'd returned to the States, he'd enjoyed the company of his fellow female soldiers, or perhaps a sister or two who visited base to see a brother. The longest relationship had lasted through one whole tour, although when Seth had returned, he'd discovered she'd gotten engaged to an attorney.

*I need someone who's here*, she'd said when he'd seen her visiting her brother on base. *You get it, right?*

He did. But now that he had returned, who was he, really? He had to admit that he didn't know more often than not.

He glanced at his watch. He still had hours yet before he'd need to get to work. After much persuasion from Lizzie, Seth had decided to start woodworking again, something he'd enjoyed as a teenager but had given up when he'd enlisted. He knew he needed something productive despite still receiving a small paycheck from the Marines.

He didn't want to be a bum by any means. It just felt like any other job—accountant, barista, construction worker—seemed pallid in comparison to being in the military. It felt so…pointless, really.

Sometimes Seth wasn't sure he was fit for anything except being a soldier.

Taking up a figurine he'd started a few days ago, he began to whittle, not entirely certain what the figurine was going to become. A horse? A dog? With a smile, he began to carve out the delicate wings of a bird—a tiny hummingbird, to be precise, caught in midflight.

CALLIE SENSED HEATH'S UNEASE, and she followed him about Rose's apartment as he paced. Rose had seen her brother agitated—to say the least—but never from something as benign as another man in her apartment. He was acting like he'd caught them naked and fooling around on the living room floor.

Rose blushed at the image. Feeling exceptionally foolish and out of sorts, she started unpacking more boxes. She needed to do something productive. She needed to stop thinking about Seth Thornton, and about *fooling around* with him.

"Do you know what you're doing?" Heath asked. He crouched down next to her. "Rose, stop. Look at me."

She glared at him. "How many times are you going to ask me that question?"

"Until you answer me with something that isn't 'I don't know.'"

She sighed. "I moved here for *you*. I was content to stay in Seattle, but you wanted me close by. I lived with you for a month until I got my own place. I have a job, an apartment. A life. What more do you want?"

"You have a place with no furniture, no bed, and barely any things. You're a waitress when you could be so much more." His tone gentled. "I haven't seen you in years. You wouldn't *let* me see you."

She looked away. She had hidden herself away from Heath. Not because he'd done something to her—quite the opposite. She'd been ashamed, and she'd wanted to lick her wounds without anyone hovering. Mostly, she'd wanted to hide from everyone and everything until maybe all of the bad would dissipate like a thick mist.

Except that wasn't how life worked. She could run, hide, avoid, deny until she reached the ends of the earth, but it would all catch up with her eventually.

She hadn't told Heath about her run-in with Rich, or how Johnny was getting impatient.

At the tender age of twenty, Rose had met Johnny Porter at a local bar, and she'd become enamored with him within two hours. Johnny had been handsome, self-assured, and he'd wanted *her*, tiny, unassuming, plain little Rose DiMarco.

After their parents' deaths, Rose and Heath had been on their own. Heath had done his best to provide for them both; he'd finished college and received his teacher's license. They'd never be rich, but it'd be a steady income. Rose had been able to attend college on a scholarship, and that was when she'd met Johnny.

But then Heath had been arrested for drug trafficking, which had been a total setup. Heath would never do such a thing. And Johnny had come to the rescue, promising to get the charges dismissed and erased. All Rose had to do was stay with him.

She'd had no idea what that would really mean. That staying would mean imprisonment in that tower she hated so much.

Heath didn't know the deal she'd made with the veritable devil. He thought she'd gotten the money some other way. She would keep it that way; she never wanted Heath to feel guilt over a decision she'd made herself.

Rose had been working to save up the money to pay Johnny back ever since she'd escaped his clutches. She'd reasoned that he'd leave her be if she could pay him back— with interest.

She was so close to having enough money. And then she could get her life back.

"I'm sorry I avoided you for so long," she said quietly. "My breakup really did me in."

"Seven years is a long time to get over a broken heart."

"Six," she murmured. "We were together a year."

She'd made the lame excuse that Johnny had broken her heart and had cheated on her. She hadn't wanted Heath to see her at her very lowest. She'd struggled with odd jobs, lived in seedy apartments, and had barely survived. But she'd clawed her way back from the horror of her past, and she refused to let anyone take advantage of her ever again.

If that meant she'd live the rest of her life alone? So be it.

"I'm not sure one less year makes a difference." Heath

smiled sadly. "I'm glad you're here, Rose. I've missed having you around."

That made her want to cry, but she choked back any tears that threatened. "I know. Although I'm not sure how you can stand to live in a town this small. *Everyone* knows you."

"It's worse when you're a teacher. The kids never ever leave you alone."

"Poor Heath. You could've been anything else, you know. A fireman. Park ranger. Tree surgeon."

He raised his eyebrows. "A tree surgeon? Now you're just making stuff up."

Rose, never one to have anyone think she was wrong, pulled out her phone to prove to her brother that tree surgeon was, in fact, a viable profession. After that, they finished unpacking her things, Callie lying down on her dog bed in the corner.

"I'd ask you to stay for dinner, but it's going to be ramen noodles for a little while before I get my paycheck," Rose admitted. At Heath's concerned look, she added, "I'm fine. Don't worry about me."

"You keep saying that, but it's not really working."

"I know this might be hard to believe, but I'm not that stupid twenty-year-old girl anymore."

He chucked her under her chin. "You still look young, and you're my baby sister. Tough luck." He looked away, his expression going serious. "Speaking of which…"

Rose really didn't want to hear where this segue was going, but Heath was too stubborn to keep it to himself. She sighed inwardly.

"About Seth Thornton. Watch yourself."

"What, does he have a cellar full of bodies somewhere?" she joked.

Heath didn't laugh. "I don't know him well, since he's been in the military until last year, but from what his brothers have told me, he's not the same guy they knew. He went through some shit; he's basically disconnected from his family entirely."

"But he came back to Fair Haven anyway?" Now Rose was even more intrigued.

"I guess. Look, just be careful. I don't want you to get hurt, okay?"

Rose barely bit back a smile. "I'm not interested in dating anyone. I've decided to become a nun, actually. Now, are you done lecturing me about the monsters under my bed, or should I get a chair and sit down?"

"You're a brat." He kissed her cheek and then said goodbye.

Rose sat on the floor next to Callie after Heath left, rubbing the dog's silky head. She'd spoken the truth when she'd said she didn't want to date. After Johnny, she *couldn't* date. She'd gone on two dates that had been disasters: one had resulted in her accidentally punching the guy in the nose, while the second had ended with her leaving the guy without a word when he'd asked her to come over to his place.

She was messed up. Broken. No guy wanted a girl who was too scared to let a guy so much as hold her hand.

"What do you think, girl? Have I made a mistake moving here?"

Callie woofed quietly and wagged her tail.

Rifling through her suitcase, Rose found the safe where she kept her most precious possessions: a ring from her mother; a watch from her father; her passport; and a wad of cash that she counted whenever she needed to find some sense of calm.

She counted the bills, knowing the amount exactly but needing to confirm the number anyway. She was so close to paying Johnny off, she could taste it. It had taken her years of saving, but by the end of the summer, she'd have the money.

The last item in her safe? A gun she'd bought the day she'd run from Johnny.

The gun was small, unassuming, yet it had provided her with peace of mind ever since she'd bought it and taken shooting lessons. She wasn't a sharpshooter by any means, but she could protect herself. Combined with Callie as her guard dog, she felt almost safe.

She knew it was an illusion, though. Until she paid Johnny off, she'd never be fully safe.

# CHAPTER THREE

"Shh, Bea is napping," Lizzie cautioned as she let Seth in. "She should be up in a half hour, though."

Seth wanted to tease his twin sister about how much she'd changed in the last year—who would've imagined Lizzie worried about waking up a baby?—but considering what his sister would do to him if he woke up the baby…

"Trent's at La Bonita until this evening. How are you? I feel like I haven't seen you in forever."

"It's been a week, Lizard."

Lizzie, with her dark hair and bright green eyes, looked like one of the Thorntons, although she and Seth only resembled each other in their hair and eye color. She was the opposite of him in every other way: slender and of average height, she was quite a bit shorter than him and had been since he'd outgrown her in junior high.

Despite having given birth only two months ago, Lizzie looked radiant. Tired, definitely, and a little harried: her hair was frizzy, and Seth saw what looked like spit-up on her t-shirt, but she was happy. After a long road of ups and downs, she and her soulmate, Trent Younger, had finally gotten back together.

Now they were married with a daughter. Seth felt old. Or maybe more left out. While his siblings married and reproduced, he was—doing what? Whittling and building tables?

"Have you been sleeping?" he asked Lizzie. Last time they'd talked, Bea hadn't exactly enjoyed sleeping through the night.

"Somewhat. We're getting three to four hours without her waking up. It could be worse. At least she isn't screaming all day long."

"Do babies do that?"

Lizzie laughed. "You're such a guy. Yeah, some babies are colicky and scream no matter what you do."

At the thought, Seth paled. He'd been to war, seen men die, yet the thought of an infant screaming nonstop for hours every day? He shuddered.

Lizzie cocked her head to the side. "Oh, she's up. I'll be right back."

Seth hadn't heard a thing, but he put it down to mother's intuition. A few minutes later, Lizzie returned with Bea in her arms. At two months old, Bea still had blue eyes, although they'd turned a little grayer in the past few weeks. She had a shock of dark hair sticking from the crown of her head and the softest skin Seth had ever felt.

And clearly she was wide awake and in no hurry to go back to sleep.

"That's your uncle Seth. Remember him? Here, can you hold her while I get us some tea?"

Seth took his niece without protest. He'd held her enough times not to freak out, although he still couldn't believe how tiny she was. How fragile. Gazing down at her now, he took in her long, dark eyelashes and her rosebud mouth. He traced a finger along her forehead, which made her coo. She'd been making eye contact more and more and working on lifting up her head.

Before long she'd be a teenager and sneaking out of the house to meet her boyfriend.

Seth's stomach turned. *No way is any boy getting close to my niece*, he vowed.

He let Bea hold his finger, which she quite happily gnawed on. Lizzie came back with tea for them both.

"You're going to get baby slobber all over you doing that," she warned, smiling. "We think she has a tooth coming in."

"Isn't she young for that?"

"Now you're Mr. Baby Expert? Yeah, it's early, but she wants to chew everything."

Seth smiled. "Sounds like a puppy."

They chatted, Lizzie telling him about her album sales, how Terry, her producer, wanted her to go on tour later that year but that she didn't know how to do that except to take Bea with her.

"Even by December I'll still be nursing her, at least on and off. And I'm not going to leave my kid behind for months on end. No way."

Seth didn't respond to the nursing remark. He'd learned all he ever needed to know about breastfeeding during one visit when Bea had kept kicking the blanket Lizzie had placed over her to give them both some privacy during a feeding.

"But I've been writing even more than usual, so that's good. Now that I'm getting some sleep and Bea has more of a schedule, I can think about other things besides baby, baby,

baby." Lizzie tickled Bea under her chin, which made her gurgle.

"Are you happy, Lizard?" Seth asked suddenly. He'd seen his sister at her lowest, at her most brokenhearted, and sometimes he struggled to believe she'd overcome it all.

"Of course I am. I mean, I'm tired and I wish Trent would put the toilet paper roll on correctly and not leave beard hairs in the bathroom sink, but that's life. I'm so grateful we found each other again. And made this little booger."

Lizzie scooped up Bea, giving her kisses on her chubby cheeks.

"She's pretty cute," Seth allowed.

"You hear that, Bea-Bea? Your uncle thinks you're 'pretty cute.' I think you're adorable, but he's a silly boy, so we'll let it slide."

When Bea started to fuss, Lizzie had Seth hand her a blanket nearby before starting to nurse, already getting over any self-consciousness that she might have had when she'd first started breastfeeding. It all seemed so *normal* that Seth felt guilty feeling a bit awkward about it all.

Then again, this was his sister. There were some things you didn't think about in regard to your siblings.

"Tell me what you're doing. And don't tell me that all you do is go to the lake, or walk around, or stare at the wall." Lizzie wagged a finger.

"I'm doing some woodworking, got a commission for a dining room table. Alan wants me to work with him full-time."

Alan Devinson was a middle-aged man who'd owned a small carpentry business for two decades, and he'd actually taught the woodworking class when Seth was in high school. Seth had taken to woodworking, but he'd been out of practice for so many years he hadn't been sure if he could make himself truly useful.

After some practice, though, the movements, the skills, the feeling of the different types of wood in his hands had returned to him. He was far from Alan's ability, but Alan recognized talent when he saw it.

"That's great! See, I told you it'd be worth trying out again. You were so good at it in high school."

He smiled. "High school was a long time ago."

"Was it? I mean, yes, it was, but we aren't *that* old. Sometimes I wonder if you're just an old man stuck in a twenty-seven-year-old's body."

"If I am, it's because you sucked out all of my energy."

That resulted in a small tiff, with Lizzie writing a list of every stupid thing Seth had ever done while Seth started his own list about Lizzie. By the time Trent came home, Lizzie was in the lead for Stupid Things She'd Done.

"Do you see this? What kind of a brother creates a list like this?"

She gave Trent the list, rolling her eyes. Bea had nodded off in her arms, but at the sound of her father's voice, her eyelids fluttered.

"Wait, why is 'dating Trent' on the list of stupid things?" Trent asked.

"Because it *was* stupid," said Seth.

The trio bantered, Trent and Seth ribbing each other, Lizzie rolling her eyes the entire time. Trent finally got up, kissed his wife's cheek, and said he'd be out back.

Lizzie turned her attention back to Seth, and when he saw the serious look in her eyes, he braced himself.

"You know how worried I am about you," she said quietly. "I'm glad to see you doing something, but is it enough?"

"Do we need to keep having this conversation?"

"Yes, until you give me a good answer." Her eyes creased. "What about a family, Seth? Are you going to be alone forever?"

"Trying to play matchmaker?" he quipped.

"Maybe. I mean, you don't have to get married to be happy, but you've never been a loner until you came back from your last tour. I just worry, that's all."

It was on the tip of his tongue to tell her about Rose, but that would only lead to more questions. He'd asked Rose out for drinks; that didn't mean marriage and babies. But Lizzie would get overly excited, and when things ended, she'd just be disappointed.

Better to keep his mouth shut.

*Or you just don't want to admit that Rose shot you down and probably will if you ask her again.*

That, too.

Seth stayed for dinner, and Lizzie kept adding to his list of Stupid Things, Trent contributing where he could. After they'd eaten, Seth kissed his niece goodbye, let Lizzie hug him, and took the long way back to his apartment. The moon was full, and he meandered, letting his mind go.

When he got home, the quiet of the night was soon shattered when he heard banging next door, then someone slamming a door. Listening more closely, he realized it was coming from Rose's apartment. His other neighbors were an elderly husband and wife who went to sleep at eight o'clock every evening.

He waited, listening. When he heard another noise, he left

his apartment. Knocking on her door, he called, "Rose? Rose, are you okay?"

He expected an unhappy Rose, or maybe a tearful one.

One thing he didn't expect?

Seeing Rose open the door and point a gun straight at him.

ROSE YAWNED as she walked up to her apartment. It had been a long shift: first one patron had complained about his steak being first too rare, then too overdone before giving Rose all of one dollar as a tip. Then another patron had decided to pay in spare change, forcing Rose to count out ten dollars' worth of quarters, dimes, nickels, and pennies. By the time her shift had ended, she'd been dead on her feet. Even Trent had said she looked exhausted and had ordered her to go home.

When she smelled cigarette smoke wafting near her just outside her apartment complex, she stilled. It wasn't the usual type of smoke, as it had a sweetness to it that turned her stomach. Clove cigarettes—she'd know that smell anywhere.

"Johnny," she said as she came around the corner. "Do you still smoke those disgusting things?"

Johnny Porter, now in his midthirties, had remained handsome despite the passing years. He had sandy brown hair, brown eyes, and a wiry build. But what had fascinated Rose so many years ago—what had caught her in his web—was his smile. One of his front teeth had been chipped long ago, but when he smiled, it exuded pure charm.

His smile had taken down many strong men and women.

Johnny blew out a puff of smoke, which trailed into the night air. "Hullo, Rosie. Long time no see."

Rose had her hand on her gun, which she carried in her jacket. She always carried her gun when she left her apartment.

Johnny smiled and tossed the cigarette, grinding it into the cement with his bootheel. "Aren't you pretty? Did you do your hair yourself?"

"Did you come all the way here to talk about my hair?"

"Maybe."

As he came into the light, Rose saw that he had a bruise marring his right cheek, and his lip was healing from a cut. When he noticed her looking at him, he smiled that smile that had once sent her to her knees.

Now she felt nothing at all, except a vague kind of disgust with herself for letting him take her in the way that he had.

"You're a hard girl to find, you know. You bounce from Seattle without a word, and you end up here. In little ole Fair Haven. Who would've thought? Then again, I always knew you'd go back to your brother eventually. Your dear, dear brother."

Rose's grip tightened on the barrel of her gun. Johnny tilted his head to the side, studying her. Assessing her. She refused to tremble in front of him, or let him know how much she truly hated him.

"I almost have your money," she said in a tight voice. "I just need another month or two."

At that, his smile widened until his eyes were like slits. "Didn't I tell you this isn't about the money? Keep your money. Spend it on some furniture." At her widening eyes, he just shook his head. "You know what I want, Rosie. I already told you."

"I already told you I'm never going back to you."

He clucked his tongue. "Never say never." When he took a tendril of her hair between his fingers, she barely repressed a shudder. "We had good times together, didn't we? You even told me you loved me, if I remember correctly."

"I was stupid."

His grip tightened on that strand of hair, but only slightly. He let it go with a shrug. "I'm a patient man, but I'm not that patient. Either you give me your answer, or I'll make it for you."

At that, she drew her gun from her jacket. No surprise registered on Johnny's face, although Rose saw a flicker of admiration in his eyes.

"I told you that I'll have your money, with interest. After that, we're done." She unhooked the safety; her aim was true and steady. "Because I'm not that girl anymore."

"No, you're definitely not that girl anymore. You're gorgeous when you're angry, by the way."

She didn't move, just kept her aim trained at his heart. "Get out of here before I have you arrested."

"And then have all of your brother's secrets revealed? I doubt it." He pushed the gun down, shaking his head.

Rose wanted to shoot him straight through the heart. Her finger ached to pull the trigger, to the point that her eyes watered. It could all be over in one instant.

"You're not a killer. Now, how about you stop acting like an idiot and give in?" He still had his hand on the gun, but then his fingers inched up until they gripped her wrist, his fingers digging into her skin so hard she had to stifle a gasp of pain. "How about you stop fucking with me and come back to Seattle?"

She tried to pull away, but in a swift movement, he took her gun, pulled out the bullets, and tossed them down into a nearby stairwell. He handed her back the gun with a sad smile.

"Make a decision. I'll be waiting." He moved so close to her that she could smell his clove-scented breath.

He'd once told her he smoked clove cigarettes for the novelty of them, and because he wanted people to remember him every time they met. *I am memorable, aren't I, Rosie?*

"You have two weeks. I have to go back to Seattle for some business. Lucky you. But after that?" He smiled, but there was no warmth in it. "You're mine."

Rose only moved from her spot when she heard a car driving off into the night. She knew she was trembling, but somehow it didn't register that *she* was the one shaking. She knew she was disassociating—she'd heard the word from a therapist she'd gone to all of two times when she'd had the money.

She didn't want to associate with her body, with her mind, with her memories. It made sense to separate herself, didn't it?

She didn't remember moving from that spot, or unlocking her apartment door, or going to her bedroom to load her gun again. She only came back to herself when Callie barked a warning at her. That was when she had to kneel on the floor to catch her breath. Dizziness swamped her, but mostly it was the fear that clutched at her throat until she was sure she was drowning.

She went to the kitchen, slamming cabinets. She shut her bedroom door until it shook her apartment. It was as if she needed the noise to confirm she was still *alive*. That she was still here.

When she heard the pounding on her door and then someone calling her name, she didn't hesitate. Adrenaline raced through her, and as anger burst inside her in waves, she hoped to God that it was Johnny returning so she could go through with shooting him in the heart.

"Rose, are you—?"

And without blinking an eye, she leveled her gun not at Johnny's heart this time, but at Seth Thornton's.

Seth, being the soldier that he was, didn't yell or freak out. He stilled, slowly raising his hands to show that he didn't have a weapon.

Logically, she knew he wasn't a threat, yet she couldn't lower her gun. Fear and anger filled her, and it was like she and Seth had become statues in some bizarre pantomime.

Neither moved for a long moment.

"Rose, lower the gun. I'm not going to hurt you." When Seth moved toward her, Callie growled a warning. He stayed put.

Then, once again: "Rose. Hey, it's me. Seth, your neighbor. Put the gun down."

She lowered the gun. She put the safety back on and set it on a nearby table.

"What do you want?" she asked Seth in a hoarse voice. Callie stayed by her side, her constant guard.

Seth shrugged. "Well, all things considered, I'd say you owe me a glass of something hard. Got any whiskey, by chance?"

# CHAPTER FOUR

Seth had stared down the barrel of a gun many times, but never had his potential assailant been a beautiful woman. A beautiful woman who also happened to be his neighbor.

Oddly enough, he didn't feel afraid having Rose point a gun at him: he felt pride. She knew how to handle a gun, and her stance bespoke a woman who had done a lot of practicing with the weapon in her hand.

It also told him that she'd gotten the gun for a legitimate reason.

He kept saying her name, calmly, slowly, until she returned to herself. He saw a flash of something—embarrassment?—in her eyes before she finally put down the gun and set it aside.

At his request for whiskey, she frowned, but she allowed him to come inside without further comment. Callie growled low in her throat; Seth gave the dog a wide berth. He knew what German shepherds could do when protecting their masters. There was a reason the military used them so often.

"I just have rosé," Rose said, a slight smile plying her lips finally.

"Appropriate. I'll take it."

"Really? Huh." She poured him a glass of the pink stuff in a plastic cup before pouring some for herself. "I like a guy secure enough in his masculinity to drink pink wine."

"Booze is booze. Staring down a gun tends to make a guy not so picky."

They drank in silence. Callie eventually went to lie on her bed, eyeing them both with canine alertness. Rose, however, wouldn't look at him. He'd expected an apology, or at least an explanation.

At her continued silence, he was torn between amusement and exasperation.

"You want to tell me what that was all about?" he finally asked. He leaned against the kitchen counter.

She sipped her wine. "Nope."

"Too bad. You don't get to almost shoot me and not explain."

"I thought you were someone else. That's all."

"I figured that, except that clearly this 'someone else' is a threat to you. You don't exactly level a gun at your mailman delivering you a package."

"Mailmen don't deliver at ten o'clock at night."

*No wonder Heath looked so worried about her. This girl...* He caught her gaze, and inwardly he dared her to break eye contact.

She didn't look away this time.

"You know, when I was fighting in Afghanistan, I had a fellow soldier almost shoot me. He'd been having nightmares, and when I tried to wake him up, he somehow had a gun that he pointed right at my temple." He tapped said temple. "Luckily, my friend Max talked the guy down. It was a close call, though. He was sent back to base in Germany to get a mental evaluation."

Rose pursed her lips. "Are you saying I need a mental evaluation?"

"No, I'm saying that it takes a great deal of fear to make a person do what you just did. And to be so afraid that you can't recognize who's really standing in front of you." He saw her shudder, and he marveled again at her aplomb. Most women would be sobbing at this point, wouldn't they?

"So, you have two choices here: you can tell me what's going on, or I'll stay here until you tell me what's going on."

She snorted. "Sounds like I have one choice only."

"Exactly. And I have all night."

"Look, Seth," she said with a bone-deep sigh, "I'm sorry about this. I never would've hurt you. I just got freaked out, that's all. It won't happen again."

"That's nice, but not the answer I'm looking for."

At that, she curled her lip in annoyance. "It's none of your business."

"Spoiler alert, the moment you pointed your gun at my heart, it became my business." And in a quieter voice, he added, "Does this have anything to do with your brother?"

She froze. Her eyes widened, and her breath caught. Yet she didn't crumple at his feet. Her hand trembling, she brushed strands of hair from her forehead that had fallen from her loose braid.

"How did you—?" She smiled bitterly. "Never mind, I don't want to know. It isn't about him, not directly. All I can say is that I have an ex-boyfriend who won't leave me alone. That's all."

Seth looked at her incredulously. "'That's all'? You're

scared enough to buy and learn how to use a gun because you have an ex who won't leave you alone?" Anger began to lace his voice, but when Rose stepped back from him, he forced himself to stay calm. "How long has this been going on? Did he follow you from wherever you moved from?"

"Yes, kind of. It's been going on and off for a few years now."

"Define a few years for me."

She bit her lip, which made his body heat. He stifled a groan. *Not the time to get turned on, Thornton.*

"Look, this is my problem, not yours. Thank you for wanting to help, but really, I'm fine. It's fine."

Seth wanted to shake her, or tell her she didn't have a choice and she was going to tell him exactly what was going on. But he had a feeling that Rose kept things close to the chest, and considering he'd been accused of doing the same, he couldn't fault her for it. And really, what did she know about him? Very little. He was a neighbor who had helped her move, who had helped her against a guy trying to accost her—

"Wait, was your ex the one trying to mess with you last month?" He frowned. "That tiny asshole?"

That made her laugh in surprise. "Rich? God, no. No, he's one of Johnny's guys." After saying her ex's name aloud, though, she shut her mouth, clearly having said too much.

"So Johnny is stalking you and, I'm assuming, threatening you." The anger returned, and he imagined all kinds of scenarios where he took out this Johnny on his own. Made Johnny beg for forgiveness before beating the shit out of him. Made sure that that look of fear in Rose's eyes never returned.

He stepped closer to Rose, and he heard her quiet inhale.

"If you think I'm going to let you deal with this on your own —no matter how good you are with a gun—you're mistaken."

Her eyes widened. "Why? Why does it matter to you? You don't know me."

"Maybe I want to get to know you better." He hadn't planned on saying that, but it was true. He wanted to get to know her. He wanted her with a desire that almost sent him to his knees.

She was beautiful, but it wasn't just that. She had spirit, and she refused to back down. Even if it frustrated him, it also intrigued him.

And as if he'd let a woman deal with a shitty, violent ex on her own.

He saw her swallow, her throat working. She started to tremble, and when he wanted to touch her, she stepped away. She played with her braid in obvious agitation.

When she refused to say anything else, he said, "I'll go to the police, if you won't. My brother is a cop, you know."

He almost laughed at her expression, considering she looked more outraged at that statement than anything else that had been said prior.

"You wouldn't. No, you can't. It would only make things worse." She steeled herself. "It would hurt not just me, but Heath. I can't tell you why—it's his story to tell. But believe me, involving the police won't help."

"Then I guess I have no choice: I'll protect you myself."

IT HAD BEEN A STRANGE EVENING, to say the least. First, Johnny; second, Seth. Pointing a gun at Seth. Seth seemingly unfazed by the whole thing. Here he stood, in her kitchen, acting like he was talking about some mundane topic. Did nothing upset the man?

Rose had barely kept her composure. Guilt filled her for having almost shot Seth, of all people, and she desperately wanted him to leave so she could lock herself in her apartment and never come out again.

But Seth wasn't going anywhere, was he? She gritted her teeth. *I'm not going to be bullied by another man—no matter how handsome he is.*

"Protect me? What, like some bodyguard?"

He lifted a shoulder. "Call it what you want."

She laughed, because it sounded so ridiculous. "Well, you can't exactly follow me around everywhere, so good luck with that. I'm not paying you."

"Call it a favor."

She stared at him incredulously. He wasn't joking. She had a feeling Seth Thornton rarely joked, and certainly not about something like this. Her throat felt dry and scratchy, and she could still smell Johnny's stupid clove cigarettes on her clothes.

"You know what?" she said, exasperated. "Do what you want. I don't have time for this. I'm tired, I had a shitty day at work, and then my ex-boyfriend shows up at my door. Then you act like Kevin Costner trying to be tough. I'm good, thanks."

She finished off her wine and set down the cup a little too forcefully, and she almost growled when she saw Seth's eyes crinkle in amusement.

"What is it with men?" she groused as she moved toward her single chair in her living room. "All they ever do is try to control me. And I'm tired of it."

Seth stepped around the kitchen island and grasped her elbow, forcing her to turn around. His grip was gentle, but his expression was not.

"I'm not interested in controlling you," he said in a low voice that sent shivers down her spine. "I'm here because you were so scared that you pointed a gun at me. I have a feeling you need more help than you're willing to say."

She stared into his green eyes, her heart pounding in her throat. She wanted, rather desperately, for him to kiss her. It was a strange reaction, all things considered, but she reasoned it was because she knew his kiss would make her forget. His kiss would make her feel safe for once.

But the ever-present fear wouldn't let her indulge herself. She thought of forceful kisses that had ended in things she'd rather forget. When she began to shake, Seth's expression gentled.

"Talk to me, princess. Won't you talk to me?"

She gasped for air. "If I talk, I'll never stop."

*If I talk, you won't want to be near me anymore.*

Was that her true fear? That everyone in her life would reject her once they knew what she'd done, even though she'd done it to save her brother?

She struggled between the desire to share her burden with Seth and the fear of his disgust.

So she said nothing, because in the end, silence was always the safest option.

"I need to go to bed," she whispered, pulling away from his grip.

His eyes roved over her face, and it was in that moment that she knew he wasn't going to let her go that easily. She wondered if part of the reason she quivered was from the knowledge that this man could mean more to her than she could ever imagine.

He brushed a finger across her cheek. "Good night," he said.

After he left, she locked the door and checked it twice, then she took her gun into her bedroom. She only fell asleep feeling the weight of it against her palm.

# CHAPTER FIVE

"Hey Rose, can you get my table?" Rebecca asked, her expression harried. Rebecca had just started at The Fainting Goat, and she tended to get overwhelmed easily.

Rose waved a hand. "Go take a break. I'll take care of them."

Rebecca sent her a grateful look and sneaked to the back, where she'd stay until Trent noticed one of his latest waitresses had disappeared. Rose enjoyed working at the local bar: Trent and his assistant manager, Landon, were fair, although they expected their employees to work hard and follow the rules. Rose had been astonished when Trent had told her that not only did his staff receive more than minimum wage, but they kept the tips they received.

Rose had almost jumped at the chance when Trent had called her and told her he had a position for her.

Despite the decent wages and tips, it still wasn't a ton of money. Although Fair Haven was a far cry from being as expensive as Seattle just south of them, the cost of living was high. Thus the reason why Rose had an apartment but no bed at the moment.

Trent generally made the rounds of all three of his restaurants weekly, although Rose had been surprised to see him in today. He usually enjoyed Saturdays with his new wife and baby.

When Trent saw her surprised face, he laughed. "Don't tell Lizzie I'm here, or she'll kill me. But Landon wants me to look over some books, and Ash is in Vancouver, the asshole."

Rose's lips twitched. Ash was Trent's younger brother, who also did his books. Rose had found Ash both ridiculously handsome and almost unknowable, with his sarcasm and banter.

And he didn't hold a candle to another man who had haunted her thoughts for weeks now.

As Rose was bringing out food for one of her tables, she spotted Lizzie with Bea. She barely stifled a laugh. Poor Trent was in for it now.

Rose had to pass by Lizzie to get to the kitchen, and Lizzie's face brightened with genuine warmth upon seeing her. Rose had found Lizzie Thornton—now Lizzie Younger— extremely intimidating, given that she was a real-life pop star. Rose loved Lizzie's albums and had barely stopped herself from turning into some teenage fan girl. But Lizzie had a sweetness about her that made you instantly comfortable in her presence. It helped that she usually had Bea with her, who was easily the cutest baby in existence.

"Is my stupid husband here?" Lizzie asked. At Rose's expression, she sighed. "He promised he wouldn't come in tonight. It's date night."

"I think he just needed to check something," Rose said. When Bea noticed Rose, she gave her a toothless smile.

"Here, will you hold her so I can knock some sense into Trent? I'll just be a minute."

Rose hesitated, but then Lizzie placed the warm bundle in her arms, and Rose was instantly smitten.

"Excellent. You're the best," Lizzie said before going into the back to find her husband.

Bea could just hold her head up at this point, although since Rose knew very little about infants, she made sure to keep a hand under the baby's head just in case as she lifted her to her shoulder. Bea smelled like baby powder and that mysterious scent babies had that lured you in. Rose laughed when Bea tried to gnaw on her shoulder, although if she weren't so cute, she'd be more dismayed at the drool stain on her t-shirt.

She caught Bea's gaze, and she couldn't help but marvel at how much Bea looked like Seth. Maybe it was the eyes, or the dark hair, or maybe she was just seeing things. Babies tended to look like everybody and nobody at this stage.

Her stupid heart clenched at the thought of Seth and babies, and she pushed away the thought ruthlessly before it wiggled deeper into her heart.

"Is there something you need to tell me?" Heath approached with a smile.

Rose rolled her eyes. "This is Bea. You've met Lizzie and Trent's daughter, right?"

"I have, but I didn't know you'd become a babysitter for them."

"I'm just holding her until Lizzie gets back." Bea cooed and reached for Rose's nose, which made her laugh. "More importantly, what are you doing here?"

"Getting a beer with Harrison and Caleb. When do you get off work?"

"Not until ten," she said.

"Too bad, otherwise I'd ask you to join us."

Considering how much the Thorntons looked alike, the last thing Rose wanted was to hang around guys who looked just like Seth. She smiled at Bea, laughing again when the baby did anything remotely adorable.

Lizzie returned, Trent in tow, and Rose handed Bea over. Bea started to fuss instantly.

"Oh no, she definitely loves you now," Lizzie said. She bounced Bea in her arms. "Rose has to get back to work. Come on, I bet you're just hungry."

Trent nodded at Heath as he left with his wife and daughter. After Heath saw Harrison and Caleb enter, he told Rose he'd see her later. Rose went into the back to fetch Rebecca, who'd definitely taken a way longer break than necessary.

The Fainting Goat always got busy on Saturdays, and this evening was no different. About a half hour later, Sara, Megan, and Jubilee entered. Sara was Harrison's wife—and, Rose couldn't help but notice, cradling what looked like a growing baby bump—while Megan was Sara's sister and Caleb's wife. Jubilee was the youngest Thornton.

When Caleb saw the women, he waved at them. "Come sit with us!"

Megan put her hands on her hips. "What are you doing here?"

"Getting a drink, like I told you."

"I don't remember you telling me that."

Caleb pulled up a chair for her, kissing her cheek. "You just weren't listening, as usual."

For that, he was pinched, and Rose found herself helping Rebecca serve the table of six. As the two singles, Heath and Jubilee sat next to each other, and Rose couldn't help but notice that Jubilee would not look Heath in the face.

And Heath? Her normally easygoing older brother seemed…distracted. Rose narrowed her eyes. *That's interesting. Very interesting.*

As she filled Jubilee's glass with water, the girl seemed not to notice Rose at all, but instead stared straight ahead. As Rose moved to Heath, Heath grabbed a napkin from the stand in the center of the table right at the same time as Jubilee reached for her glass of water. Their two arms bumped, and Jubilee reacted like she'd been burned. In something that seemed straight out of a sketch comedy show, Jubilee dropped her glass, dumping most of the ice-cold water in Heath's waiting lap.

Heath jolted; Jubilee cried, "Oh!" And Rose had to shove her fist in her mouth so she didn't laugh too loudly at her brother's discomfiture.

"Oh my God, I'm so sorry," Jubilee kept saying. Heath had stood up, and Jubilee was handing him napkin after napkin.

Heath just shook his head. "It's fine. It's just water. It's fine."

Jubilee, clearly not thinking, pressed a napkin against the water spot—right on Heath's upper thigh.

She snatched her hand away, a bright red blush on her cheeks, a second later. Heath's own cheeks looked a little red, and he muttered something about going to the bathroom before stalking away.

The rest of the party had missed everything except Heath leaping up like a scalded cat.

"What was that about?" Megan asked.

"I spilled water on Heath." Jubilee sounded miserable, like she'd accidentally run over his dog.

Harrison snorted. "He'll be fine. Don't worry, Jubi. It's just water."

"I know, but he'll be all wet now—"

Rose leaned down to Jubilee. "I'll get him a towel, plus there are dryers in the bathroom. No worries."

Jubilee gave her a grateful smile, although when Rose went to the kitchen to get some dish towels, she couldn't help but notice Jubilee rushing to the women's bathroom.

Well, that had been memorable.

Rose knocked on the door to the men's bathroom. "Heath, it's me. I have some towels."

Each bathroom was just a single stall, and Heath opened the door after a few moments. He seemed to have regained his composure, although when Rose saw the giant wet spot on his crotch, she started laughing.

He rolled his eyes. "Are you five? Give me those towels."

She followed him inside the bathroom and locked the door.

"Do you really want to see me take off my pants?" he asked.

"No, but I just wanted to ask you: what is Jubilee Thornton to you?"

She'd never seen her brother go so...still. Completely frozen. It was like time stood completely still. Rose had never understood the expression, "you could hear a pin drop," but in this instance? You could hear a pin drop.

He stared at her via his reflection in the mirror. "She's nothing," he ground out.

"You know, it's funny to me that you get to grill me about my nonexistent love life, yet when I ask you, you refuse to say a thing." She tapped her lip. "I think that's called something. Oh, what's the word? Hyp—hyp—hypocrisy?"

He growled. "Go away."

"I'll just say this," she said with a wide smile, "be careful of those Thorntons."

He swore under his breath at her parroting his words, and before he could throw something at her, she ran from the restroom. She did hear some more swearing from inside before she returned to work.

She might be Heath's younger sister, but that didn't mean Rose wouldn't use any leverage against her brother whenever he tried to tell her what to do.

Some hours later, Rose walked home, yawning multiple times as she walked the few blocks back to her apartment. She didn't have money for a car, although luckily, she didn't live too far from her work.

Despite her tiredness, she remained alert to any strange noises or movements. She wasn't stupid: she knew Johnny or Rich or some other crony could appear at any time. Johnny might have said he was going to Seattle, but that didn't mean a damn thing.

When a figure appeared from the shadows only feet from her door, she reached inside her jacket to pull out her gun. Until she realized it was Seth.

"Now you must be stalking me," she groused. She was halfway tempted to point her gun at him anyway.

He had his hands up, although he didn't look scared. Of

course not. Rose was fairly certain nothing scared Seth.

"What are you doing out here?" she asked when he said nothing.

He shrugged. "I couldn't sleep. It's nice out. I thought I'd say hi to my neighbor when she got home. The usual."

"Uh-huh. Well, you've said it, and now I'm saying good-bye. I need to let Callie out before I go to bed."

"Then I'll walk with you."

She wanted to stomp her foot, she was so frustrated, but she had a feeling that would only make it worse. Sighing, she went to get Callie, ignoring Seth even as he walked alongside her.

Callie, to Rose's annoyance, decided she was not going to do her business quickly. The dog wanted to sniff every bush and every mailbox, and despite Rose's continued commands, Callie ignored her entirely.

"Do you carry your gun everywhere?" Seth asked quietly as Callie sniffed a hydrangea.

"Why do you want to know?"

"Curiosity."

"Yes, for the most part. I'm legal, if that's what you're worried about."

That made him smile. "I wasn't. You seem to know how to handle a gun regardless."

"You sound surprised."

"No, merely impressed."

Pride filled her, and she ducked away so he wouldn't see her smile. Coming from a military man, she considered that to be a high compliment.

She suddenly wished she could tell him the reason why she carried a gun—why her memories forced her to protect herself the best way she knew how. Under the night sky, the moon heavy and low, it seemed as if they were the only two people in the entire world.

"So what happens now? Is this how you're going to live your life forever?"

His voice was calm, like he was asking the time, yet she felt the tone stiffen her shoulders. She didn't need another man judging her for her choices. She had Heath for that, thank you very much.

"Here's a real question," she countered, "why do you care?"

Seth didn't answer right away, and Rose barely restrained herself from looking away from his intense gaze.

Finally, he muttered, "I don't know."

Callie did her business, and Rose brushed by Seth to return to the apartment. They'd only walked a block, although it had felt much farther.

"Rose."

He caught her by the elbow, forcing her to slow down. Her back was to him, yet she felt his touch like a brand. She gripped Callie's leash harder.

"I don't know why I care," he admitted into the night air, "but I do. I can't explain it."

She let out a laugh. "Maybe you should figure that out first."

He brushed his other hand down her arm until he embraced her from behind. Now Rose trembled, and she felt her body go hot and cold at the same time. His breath heated her cheek.

"You feel it too. I know you do." His stubble brushed her cheek. "Tell me I'm wrong, princess."

"Don't call me that." Her voice was barely above a whisper.

He turned her head so she met his gaze. Although he had his arms around her, she had the feeling that if she pushed him away, he'd let her go. It was that realization that burst something inside her, something she couldn't yet understand.

When he bent down and kissed her, she was certain her heart would explode inside her chest. He tasted like spice and something she couldn't identify, and within a moment the kiss turned heated, like a fire catching on dry tinder. She opened her mouth to his invasion, and his grip tightened around her waist.

Rose had been kissed before: some kisses had been good, others had been worth forgetting. This kiss, though, turned her inside out. Her heart beat in her ears; a flush traveled from her chest to her cheeks until she was thankful for the darkness around them. She moaned as he kissed her, licking inside her mouth, making her tremble even harder.

When Callie yanked on the leash, Rose returned to herself. Turning, she pushed Seth's hands away. Like she'd thought, he let her go.

"I need to take Callie inside," she explained. Callie, for her part, just wagged her tail and didn't seem at all concerned about going inside. Rose tugged on the leash until Callie got up to follow her.

Seth didn't say anything as she left him standing there. She heard him go inside his apartment, and she listened as he walked around. She wished he would go to sleep, because until he did, she'd never be able to close her eyes.

But when she did finally fall asleep, all of her dreams were of Seth anyway.

CHAPTER SIX

Seth hated the dreams the most.

They always started innocuously enough: he was back in the deserts of Afghanistan, the heat and the sand palpable. He heard his fellow soldiers laughing and joking around as they returned from some mission. Seth had moved up the ranks to corporal by the time he'd gone on inactive duty, and although he hadn't been in charge of anyone, he had acted like a mentor to the newbies by the time he'd started his second tour.

In this dream, Seth watched as his best friend and fellow corporal Max Meyers waved at him to join him. They were in the middle of the desert, and Seth didn't know what Max wanted to show him. He jogged up to Max, who pointed to something in the sand.

"I can't see anything," Dream Seth said, confused.

Max grinned. Max had a smile that you'd never forget, his teeth crooked yet his grin infectious. He was the jokester of their group, always trying to keep people's spirits up. Seth had found Max annoying when he'd first joined, but through sheer force of will, Max had gotten Seth to be his friend.

Dream Max pointed at some spot in the sand. "Can't you see it? It's right there."

"What's right there?"

"Seriously? Come on, Seth, you're pulling my leg here."

Seth was about to tell his friend to fuck off when Max stepped forward onto the spot. Then, before Seth could warn Max, or warn anyone around them, the spot exploded.

The sound was deafening. Seth flew into the air, and it was like time had stopped. When he finally landed on his back, the breath leaving his body, he felt the spray of blood on his face. He tried to scream Max's name, but his voice was caught in his throat.

Crawling, unable to see with the smoke and the sand obscuring his vision, Seth found something warm. It was an arm, slick with blood. As Seth's vision cleared, he saw in horror that it wasn't Max: it was Rose.

Rose, lying in the sand, bleeding her life away. She gasped something, and Seth tried to get her to stay still and quiet. He yelled, but it came out as a hoarse groan. And then, right before his eyes, Rose closed her eyes and breathed her last.

The scream caught in Seth's throat emerged as a shout that woke him from a sound sleep. Gasping for air, his entire body covered in a cold sweat, Seth took in lungfuls of air. His heart beat so fast it felt like it would beat out of his chest.

It was a dream. Just a dream.

He wondered if he was going to puke. Sometimes he did, depending on the nightmare. Other times he lay in bed, not wanting to return to sleep. Having your dreams haunt you made sleep unbearable.

Seth rose from his bed, the sheets damp with sweat, and he stumbled to the bathroom to take a shower. He let the water run until it went cold, but even then, he felt dirty.

This had been the first time his dreams had featured Rose. He couldn't stop seeing her dead in the sand, her life bleeding away as he could do absolutely nothing for her.

It was close to five a.m. Seth started a pot of coffee and sat down on the couch, knowing he'd never get back to sleep.

Seth had seen Lizzie fall apart after she'd gotten pregnant with Trent's baby and then subsequently miscarried. Seth hadn't known about the pregnancy until Trent had called him one night in February, telling Seth that he was afraid Lizzie might die from her miscarriage.

Seth had driven to Seattle in a terrified trance. The only thing that had kept him from losing it was the desire to punch the living daylights out of Trent for doing this to his twin sister.

Lizzie and Trent had broken up after that, and Lizzie had run away to be a musician, abandoning not only Trent, but Seth, too. Seth had been more hurt by her abandonment than he'd ever admitted to anyone. He and Lizzie, as twins, had done everything together as children and teenagers. Then Trent had entered the picture, and everything had been destroyed.

Seth had worked a few jobs in Fair Haven before moving to Seattle, not wanting to hear his parents complain about his throwing his life away. He had a few friends from high school working in Seattle, and he'd moved in with them. Sometimes there were women, but mostly, Seth struggled to find a purpose.

He'd never been a great student. He'd enjoyed woodworking, but after Lizzie had left, somehow he couldn't do that anymore. Maybe it was because she'd encouraged him to do it in the first place.

Then he'd gotten a knock on his door from a recruiter that had changed his life.

Seth had joined the Marines just short of his twenty-first birthday, serving three tours in five years. He'd moved up the ranks, and he'd quickly become close friends with a number of other Marines. Max had been his closest friend.

But then Max had been killed by an IED during Seth's last tour, and everything about his involvement with the Marines seemed pointless. Max had left a wife and little girl behind, but worst of all, Seth had survived when Max had not.

Seth had walked away with only some cuts and bruises, but Max had been too close to the IED. He'd been killed instantly.

So Seth had told his CO, Staff Sergeant Felix Loyd, that he was going on inactive duty instead of signing up for another tour, despite the fact that he'd have been close to attaining sergeant status if he'd stayed on active duty another year or two.

Sergeant Loyd hadn't been happy with Seth's decision. He'd called it a total waste. "You're one of my best and brightest," he'd said. "What the hell are you going to do back in Nowhere, Washington?"

And in a way, Sergeant Loyd had been right. Seth hadn't known what he'd do back here in Fair Haven.

He drank his coffee, and then around seven o'clock, he got dressed and went down to the shop to get some work done.

Alan wasn't there yet, but Seth didn't mind. He had a table he wanted to finish, and although Seth appreciated

Alan's input, sometimes it was easier not to have the old man hovering.

He didn't even hear Alan enter, he was so deep in his work, and after he'd finished the last leg of the table, Alan gave him an appreciative slap on the shoulder.

"Great work, son. I'm impressed." Alan inspected the table. Although Seth called him Old Man, Alan was no more than fifty. His gray beard lent him an older air, and Alan had embraced the title without protest.

Seth stood up, wiping his forehead. "Thanks. I need to polish it up, but it should be done by tomorrow."

"I'm still impressed you could return to woodworking after years of not doing it and be this good. I'm not sure even I could do that."

Seth shrugged, embarrassed. He was so used to the military, with its no-nonsense commands and lack of straightforward praise, that hearing Alan's compliments now made him uncomfortable.

"At this rate, I'll be hiring you full-time." Alan gave him an assessing look. "Unless you have other plans?"

"Not particularly."

"Excellent. We'll talk about it later. I need to finish up this chair today."

By the afternoon, Seth had almost forgotten about the nightmare that had awoken him that morning. Working with his hands, feeling the grain of each piece of wood, sent him into a kind of trance. He'd forgotten how much he'd enjoyed this work.

His idyll ended, though, when his phone rang and he saw it was none other than his CO calling him. Seth frowned. What the hell did Sergeant Loyd want?

Seth knew very well that, even though a reservist could be called up at any time, generally speaking, it was pretty rare. Yet seeing Sergeant Loyd's name flash on his phone caused him to feel—panicked? Excited? He didn't know how to identify this particular emotion.

"This is Thornton," he answered, stepping outside for some privacy.

"Corporal, hello—how's it going? Where are you again? Bellingham?"

"Fair Haven."

"Right. Never been there. I wanted to call you because I have an opportunity that I thought you'd be perfect for."

Seth leaned against the wall of the building, his heart hammering, wondering what the hell Sergeant Loyd had in mind this time.

"We need more guys—guys like you, Thornton—and I've wracked my brain to find somebody else, but you're the man I need. I could get you reinstated to active like that if you accepted." Seth could hear him snap his fingers. "Then you'd be on tour again by October."

Seth couldn't believe it. It was one thing to be called up again while on inactive duty; it was another to have a choice in the matter.

"What's the job?" he asked.

Sergeant Loyd gave him the lowdown, telling him again that Seth was one of his best guys, and if he took this last tour, Seth could be promoted to sergeant if he wanted.

"I know you're on inactive, but I told you that was a total waste. I think you know it, too."

"When do you need my answer?"

"The sooner the better. Let's say by July fifteenth. That's when I have to turn in my paperwork."

Seth assured Sergeant Loyd he'd give him his answer by then, and then he stood, staring at nothing, as he thought. He couldn't help but agree with his CO: what was he doing in Fair Haven? Woodworking and hanging around? He'd excelled in the Marines, moving up the ranks with ease, and the only reason he'd decided not to take a fourth tour was because he'd thought he was done. Max's death had changed his outlook: life was such a fragile thing. Could he really test the limits of his own mortality a fourth time?

But now that he was basically a civilian again, he felt lost. Adrift.

Then he thought of Rose, of her pointing a gun at him, and his vow to keep her safe. He rubbed the back of his neck. What would happen if he left her, and this ex-boyfriend of hers hurt her? Or worse?

The thought was unbearable. Even though he'd only known her a short time, she'd affected him deeply. She'd made him want to do more than just drift along in life without any purpose.

And what if another tour ended up being his last?

IF ROSE HAD KNOWN that Seth Thornton, her seemingly unassailable neighbor, suffered from nightmares just like she did, she might have just laughed. It was too ridiculous, too melodramatic.

But that night, she didn't know of Seth's dreams. She only

knew of her own, and she wished that she could be rid of them once and for all.

She always dreamed the same dream: the day when Johnny had brought her to his apartment and told her he had a deal for her. She'd been all of twenty, naïve and sheltered, and Johnny had charmed her the moment she'd met him. He was handsome and witty, and he told her she was beautiful.

When you grow up with a brother and no parents, and that same brother tries to hide you from the world in his best effort to keep you safe, it ironically creates a situation where you become vulnerable to people. People like Johnny.

She knew this dream well. Johnny handed her a glass of wine before touching her cheek. She trembled and could barely contain her tears, because her brother had been arrested for drug charges that would send him to prison for a long time if he was convicted. She knew he was innocent; he would never jeopardize his future like that, or hers. He was going to be a teacher, for God's sake. What kind of a teacher gets arrested for dealing heroin?

"Don't cry," Johnny soothed. He lounged in a chair across from her, his legs crossed. "I've got it all worked out."

She gasped in relief. "How? Do you know who did it?"

He shook his head regretfully. "No, but I know people, and I can get your brother released and the charges dropped and erased." He snapped his fingers. "Just like that. But I need something from you."

Her gut twisted at the tone of his voice, but Johnny had been kind to her. He wanted to help her. She wanted to believe he could set everything right.

"I'll do anything," she breathed.

He smiled. Rising, he sat next to her and set his arm on

the back of the couch behind her. He didn't touch her, but he didn't need to. She felt the gesture in her heart: it was a gesture of ownership.

She gripped her wineglass harder.

"If you want your brother to go free, you're mine. Do you understand?"

"I'm already your girlfriend."

His lips quirked. "Yes, you are." He brushed her throat with his fingers. "But you won't let me touch you. Still a virgin, aren't you, Rosie?"

She blushed scarlet, looking away. He leaned forward to kiss her shoulder.

"Your end of the deal is this: you're mine to do with what I want. You don't get to say no, because then I'll have your brother arrested again and thrown in jail for the rest of his life." Johnny's voice had hardened with each word, until Rose wanted to jump off the couch and run.

Fear coursed through her, until the wine in her glass splashed onto her thigh.

"What do you say?" he asked, his voice quiet yet lethal. "Yourself, or your brother? Your dear, dear brother, who took care of you when no one else would."

She knew what her answer was. What it had to be. Setting the wineglass on the table in front of her, she began to take her hair down from its braid.

And Johnny smiled.

~

SHE AWOKE with a scream lodged in her throat. She always

did. The scream could never be let out, because Johnny wanted that. He wanted her to scream.

Her head in her hands, she whispered the litany she told herself whenever she had this nightmare.

*You're free. You're here. He's gone. He's not going to hurt you anymore.*

If only that were true.

Callie followed her into the bathroom. Rose washed her face and considered taking a shower, but decided she'd rather sit and watch Bob Ross to soothe herself.

It was ridiculous, but she loved Bob Ross's voice, his happy little trees. Only joy could be found in his paintings, those hotel paintings of landscapes. Rose sometimes considered taking up painting, but she had a feeling her paintings wouldn't be full of happy little trees.

They'd be full of darkness, and shadows, and things better left buried six feet under.

She heard a noise next door, and the reminder of Seth Thornton made her pull her blanket closer around her shoulders. She almost laughed. What would he think about what she'd done? The deal she'd made with the devil to save her brother?

She thought of the kiss, the way he'd said her name. She wanted him to touch her as much as she wanted him to leave her alone.

Seth would think she was a fool, most likely. She knew very well how stupid she'd been. She'd thought she was being brave and honorable and saving her brother, but what did it mean when you sacrificed your own well-being for someone you loved? You lost yourself in the process.

So one person dies, anyway. Maybe not physically, but

spiritually. Part of her had died that moment Johnny had touched her.

She pushed the memories aside. Callie pushed her nose against her palm, giving doggy comfort. Rose smiled. She didn't cry—not anymore. She'd cried enough for five people.

All she wanted to do was repay Johnny the money he had spent to get Heath's name free and clear. And then she'd get a life of her own.

She fell asleep to the sounds of Bob Ross painting a mountain, and her dreams weren't nightmares this time. They were just as unsettling, however.

She was in Seth's apartment—she didn't know what it looked like, but her imagination supplied shadowy pieces of furniture. The walls were bright colors, which she thought was strange.

Then Seth emerged from his room without a shirt, and although she'd never seen him shirtless, she knew her imagination wasn't overblown here. He was cut like a Greek god, and her mouth went dry with sheer lust.

When he touched her hair, tipping her head back, she didn't hesitate. She closed her eyes as he kissed her. It was like the kiss outside, yet it wasn't. It possessed an intensity that shocked her to the tips of her toes. She moaned as he thrust his tongue inside her mouth, licking and searching, and she wished he was inside of her in other ways. She wanted him to make her forget.

He picked her up and carried her to his room, never breaking the kiss. When they fell onto his bed together, she laughed, but then they were both naked—as dreams tended to do, without any logical reason—and when he pushed her legs apart, she wanted to protest. She couldn't move or speak. She gripped his hair as he touched her, torn between what she wanted and what she feared.

And when he had almost pushed inside her, he disappeared into a mist, leaving her all alone.

She awoke a second time with her heart pounding and her entire body on edge. With a sigh of resignation, she touched her heated sex, not surprised by the slickness she found there. And as she came against her fingers in mere moments, Seth's name trembled on her lips.

# CHAPTER SEVEN

"Why did I agree to get up this early just to see you?" Rose joked as she barely stifled a wide yawn.

Heath grinned. "It's only nine a.m."

"You're a morning person, I'm not." She yawned again, and Heath laughed.

Rose had agreed to meet Heath for coffee that Sunday at The Rise and Shine, the bakery Megan Thornton—née Flannigan—owned and ran. Rose had only been here a few times; working at The Fainting Goat, she tended to get up late and return home in the wee hours of the morning.

"I'm not a morning person," Heath replied, "but I've been getting up early for work so many years now that I can't break the habit."

"I've never had that problem."

"Why does that not shock me?"

Rose stuck out her tongue right as Jubilee Thornton placed their two coffees and muffins in front of them. "Cinnamon latte for you," she said as she handed the drink to

Rose, "and a latte with an extra shot for you. Just how you like it," she said to Heath.

Rose suddenly felt more awake than she had been just a second ago. So not only did her brother come here often enough for Jubilee to know his order, but she made a point to remember said order.

"I heated up your muffins, too," Jubilee said. She blushed at Heath's eyebrow raise.

"Oh, you didn't need to," he said, but at her embarrassed expression, he added hastily, "Thank you, though."

Rose watched as she was completely ignored by her brother and by Jubilee, who both seemed to have stepped into their own little world. What was it about these Thorntons? Rose mused. She began to eat her muffin in silence, the warm, buttery sweetness almost making her moan out loud.

Jubilee tucked a tendril of her dark hair behind her ear. She was a beautiful girl, with her dark hair and creamy skin. She looked like her siblings, although she was smaller than her brothers and sister. Rose had only run into Jubilee a few times, and it was difficult not to like her, with her infectious smile and sweet manner.

Right now, that smile had fled, and Jubilee seemed at a loss for words. To Rose's immense amusement, her brother's cheeks were slightly red.

She tossed a large bite of muffin into her mouth, chewed, and decided to give them a reprieve.

"These muffins are amazing," Rose said. "Do you make them or does Megan?"

"Megan, for the most part, but I help. I made this batch, actually."

"I wish I could bake. I just burn things or set off the smoke alarm."

Heath seemed to shake off his trance. "Didn't you set a quesadilla on fire once when we were kids?"

"I was ten!"

"Yeah, but who sets a quesadilla on fire?"

Jubilee laughed, and it sounded like bells tinkling. If she weren't so nice, Rose would almost be liable to hate her. She had a distinct feeling Jubilee Thornton had never had to deal with anything terrible in her whole life. She'd lived a cushy existence, with her beautiful, rich family.

"I'll let you two go. Enjoy." Jubilee sent one last shy smile toward Heath before she left them to eat in silence.

Rose wanted to grill Heath about Jubilee, but her brother had a sixth sense when it came to what she was thinking. Before she could say a word, he asked, "How's work? Your apartment?"

She heard the words *your new neighbor* underneath the question. Tearing apart her muffin, she said, "Good. Fine. Nothing much to tell. Trent threw out a guy last night who got so drunk that he tried to kiss Lizzie, thinking she was his ex-girlfriend."

Heath's eyes widened. "Shit."

"Yeah, shit. Lizzie was laughing because the guy was so trashed, and he fell down in front of her before he could touch her. But Trent was *pissed*." She shook her head. "Never mess with the boss's wife."

"But that's it? Nothing else to tell?"

She wanted to laugh, but it would probably turn into a sob. She wished she could tell Heath everything about Johnny, and about how he'd given her a deadline to "make up her mind." A shiver went down her spine.

She wanted to tell him, and yet… looking at him now, seeing how he cared for her, would he still want her once he knew the truth? Heath tended to see things as very black and white. If he knew what his baby sister had done for him…

She didn't want to think about it.

So she forced a smile onto her face and replied, "When I'm not working, I walk Callie. Or read. I should probably learn how to cook. Can you die from eating ramen noodles too much?"

That made Heath frown. "Rose, if you need help—"

She held up a hand. "I'm fine. I'm joking." Leaning toward him, she said, "I have a question for you."

"Do I want to know?"

"Yes. Well, I want to know. What was that all about?" She gestured toward the direction Jubilee had gone.

Heath feigned ignorance. "What was what about?"

"Oh, come on. You, Jubilee Thornton. Those heart-eyes between you. It was like some anime."

"I have no idea what you're talking about, because there's nothing between us. She's my best friend's little sister."

"Because you're *so* old?" She rolled her eyes. "You're not even thirty. She's not some girl fresh out of high school. It wouldn't be creepy."

"Thank you," he said wryly. Then he sobered. "Even then, there's nothing there. Don't make mountains out of molehills."

"Now, that's unfair—"

"Leave it, Rose." At her shocked look, he added more

kindly, "It's nothing. Even if there is something, nothing could happen. End of story."

She wanted to point out that that made zero sense, but she knew when to leave things well enough alone. When they'd been younger, she would've teased him mercilessly until he'd finally lost his temper, which was rare for him.

Heath had always been the calm one, the capable one. He'd kept a roof over their heads after their parents had died. Their father had been killed in a car accident when Rose had only been three, while their mother had died of breast cancer when Rose was fourteen. The only fortunate part of their mother's death had been that she'd died after Heath had turned eighteen and could become Rose's guardian. Rose had been terrified that they'd be placed in foster care when they'd learned of their mother's diagnosis.

Heath had worked odd jobs, and although they didn't always have enough to eat, they'd persevered. With some scrimping and saving, along with Rose insisting that she contribute, Heath had been able to go to the University of Washington to get his teaching degree, a dream he'd had since he'd been a child.

Then Johnny—and everything that had come along with him—had happened.

Rose gazed at her muffin and felt sick to her stomach. Her latte was too sweet now, and the muffin was like a ball of lead.

"Do you remember when I brought home those four kittens?" she said, desperate to lighten the mood.

Heath grinned. "Yes, and you refused to let me take them to the shelter."

"They would've put them to sleep!"

"They were mangy little things covered in fleas."

"They were adorable."

They reminisced as the morning passed, talking about only the happy memories. They never talked about Heath's arrest, or about when Rose had disappeared and refused to talk to Heath for years. They didn't talk about the difficult things, because sometimes you need a respite from the shadows of the past.

Or perhaps, Rose thought sadly, they were both too scared to be honest with each other.

"When do you have to go back to work?" she asked as she finished up her latte. They'd talked so much it had gotten cold.

"Not until mid-August, mostly for meetings. The kids don't come back until after Labor Day." He smiled, and Rose's heart constricted. She'd missed seeing Heath with his first class and hearing about it all.

Heath had always wanted to be a teacher, ever since his favorite teacher ever, Mrs. Dunby, had inspired him in the fourth grade. Heath had a patience with kids that Rose admired; she certainly didn't have it.

"I can't imagine teaching fifth graders," she said. "That just seems so young."

"Not that young. It's better than kindergarten: at least in fifth grade, everyone's potty-trained and mostly capable of holding a conversation."

They laughed, and Heath told her about how he'd started taking his class on nature walks around Fair Haven, pointing out local flora and fauna. The kids had loved it, and everyone looked forward to having Mr. DiMarco for fifth grade. It helped that he was handsome: the girls all loved him and would blush when he'd smile at them.

"I'm glad you're happy. You were meant to be a teacher." Rose smiled as Heath rubbed his neck in embarrassment.

"It almost didn't happen." He seemed far away right then, and she knew they were both thinking about how it had almost ended so quickly. She closed her eyes for a brief second before pushing away the memories.

Heath walked Rose home a few hours later, neither of them saying much. The sun shone brightly, the trees bursting with color. Rose watched a seagull glide across the sky before landing unceremoniously on the corner of an apartment complex's dumpster.

She laughed. "What did you used to call seagulls?"

Heath looked a little startled. She wondered how far away his thoughts had been. "Seagulls? I think I called them trash parrots."

"That's right! Trash parrots. I loved that."

He smiled, slinging an arm around her shoulders.

That was how they ran into Seth only ten minutes later. When Heath spotted Seth, he stiffened, his arm drawing her close. Seth looked wary, and Rose couldn't help but think of them both as dogs, circling the same bone.

*If I'm lucky, they won't pee on me to mark their territory*, she thought wryly.

Seth eyed Heath DiMarco, while Heath's expression was one of open hostility. Seth didn't know what Heath's problem was: he'd done nothing to merit that kind of look. And he wasn't the one letting his sister live in an apartment without a damn bed while he sat in his cushy house.

Well, cushy apartment, maybe. It wasn't like teachers made a ton of money.

"Hi, Seth," Rose said.

She glanced at Heath, and Seth almost laughed when she rolled her eyes.

"Hey," Heath said; Seth just nodded.

"We just saw your sister, actually, down at The Rise and Shine."

"Which one?" Seth asked.

That earned him another full eye roll. "Which do you think? The one who works there. Jubilee is so sweet. I wonder where she gets it from?" Rose batted her lashes.

Seth grunted. "My sisters are a pain in the ass," he said, his tone at odds with his words.

"Where do you work these days?" Heath inquired. "Now that you're out of the Marines."

"I do woodworking and carpentry. And I'm not totally out of the Marines."

He didn't know why Heath was irritating him so much, but there it was. Maybe because he seemed like Seth would pounce on Rose if he so much as turned his back. *You were the same way when Trent was sniffing around Lizzie*, his mind reminded him.

He told his mind to shut the hell up.

"You're not totally done? I thought you were," said Rose.

"I'm on inactive duty. I could be called up at any time."

"Does that really happen?"

He hesitated. "Not usually. It's pretty rare."

At Heath's smug look, Seth barely restrained himself from punching him in the jaw. But then he saw the resemblance between the two siblings, and he realized it'd be like punching Rose in a way.

Besides, he wanted to stay on Rose's good side, right? So no punching older brothers.

At the strained silence, Rose huffed. "Well, I need to take Callie out and get ready for work. See you later, Heath." She kissed her brother's cheek, leaving the two men to stare each other down in the warm June sunshine.

Although Seth was taller than Heath, Seth had a feeling the man could put up a decent fight. There was an edge to Heath DiMarco that Seth recognized. He wasn't just some elementary school teacher, that was for sure.

"I want you to leave my sister alone," Heath said without preamble. "She's been through enough already."

So there it was. Seth schooled his expression, anger filling him. Did Heath even know what his sister had been through? That she carried a damn gun with her everywhere she went because she was so afraid?

He wanted to throw that little fact in Heath's face, but he stopped himself just in time. He didn't have a right to share what he knew was probably Rose's secret.

"Has Rose said that she wants me to leave her alone?" Seth countered.

"Not in so many words."

"That's a no, then."

Heath scowled. "Like I said: she's been through enough." He stepped closer until they were only inches apart. "I just got her back, Thornton. Don't make her run again."

Seth's brows flew up. *Now, there's a story.* "And like I said: if she tells me that she wants me to leave her alone, I will. But I don't take well to empty threats."

"They're not empty, believe me."

"And what kind of a brother are you? Letting your little sister live in an apartment without a bed? Eating probably only ramen noodles?" Seth's voice hardened. "Why act like you care when you clearly don't give a shit?"

Heath flinched, and Seth knew he'd made a direct hit. Something dark lurked in Heath's eyes, and Seth almost expected a fist to his gut. It had been a low blow.

"You think I don't know that?" Heath growled, shaking his head. "She won't accept my help. She won't accept anyone's help. What makes you think you're so different? Rose keeps to herself and she always has."

Seth instantly felt guilty, hearing the pain in Heath's voice. There was a history there that he couldn't begin to fathom. Lizzie had been the same way, when she'd been hurting: Seth had wanted to help, tried to help, but sometimes there's truly nothing a person can do.

"Just leave my sister alone. She needs to get a life for herself, not have some other guy sniffing around her and screwing her over again." Heath shook his head and went toward Rose's apartment, probably to make sure Seth didn't try anything.

Seth walked to the park he and Lizzie would go to when she'd lived with him in the apartment. Gazing off into the distance, Seth heard Heath's words over and over again, the pain—and the guilt—so obvious in them.

Seth understood pain, and he sure as hell felt guilt. He'd failed Lizzie, he'd failed Max. Was he drawn to Rose because he thought he could save her? Was she his redemption in a twisted way?

He rubbed his temples. A headache threatened to take

over; it didn't help that he couldn't stop clenching his jaw until his entire head pounded.

"I thought I'd find you here," Lizzie said quietly as she came to stand in front of him. She smiled down at him, although it was a sad smile. "What's up, buttercup?"

"Hey, Lizard. What are you doing here?"

"Trent has Bea, and I wanted to come see you, but you weren't home. I put two and two together." She gestured at the bench. "May I?"

He nodded.

He and Lizzie had been inseparable as kids: being twins, it had been like they could read each other's minds. Although Lizzie was technically older, Seth had always felt protective of her.

But now Lizzie had Trent, and she didn't need Seth protecting her, did she? He was no longer the most important man in her life.

"I'm tempted to ask you what's wrong, but I know you well enough to know that your answer is probably going to be 'nothing.'" Lizzie eyed him. "So, what's up?"

"Nothing."

She punched him, making him laugh a little.

"Come on. Tell me. It's the least I can do when I made you listen to everything with Trent last summer."

"And made me buy you a pregnancy test?" He'd never, ever forget that one.

That made her giggle. "I didn't *make* you. You offered. And look! You survived." She smiled, and Seth once again saw how happy his sister was. How content. It made his chest hurt, yet he would never begrudge her that happiness, either.

"For the first time in my life," he said slowly, staring into the horizon, "I have no idea what the fuck I'm doing."

"Welcome to the club."

"I thought leaving the Marines was a good idea, after Max..." He swallowed, struggling for a moment. Lizzie squeezed his hand reassuringly. "But what am I doing now? Nothing. I'm no good at anything except being a soldier."

"That's not true. You were an amazing Marine, and I'm so proud of you. But that doesn't mean you can't make a life for yourself here."

He shook his head. "I think sometimes I'm only suited to war."

It was his darkest fear: that he couldn't be anything but a man who knew how to kill. He'd turned into the military's efficient human machine; now, he couldn't return to his own humanity.

"You're lost right now. I was last year. I couldn't write a song to save my life." Lizzie leaned against his arm. "You'll get there. Be kind to yourself, Seth." Her tone turning sly, she added, "Maybe you should start dating."

He grunted.

"Rose DiMarco is very pretty, and she's your neighbor—"

"How did you know that?"

"I saw her when I stopped by your place. I didn't even know Heath had a sister," she mused. "If it makes a difference, I approve."

"Thanks, I think." Seth wished he could tell Lizzie everything about Rose—about her courage, her spunk, her fear— but he bit his tongue. It almost seemed like a betrayal to talk about her right now. Or maybe he just wanted to keep her all to himself, because he feared what would happen if he admitted how much she'd captivated him.

Rising, he put out a hand. "Come on, let's go get something to eat. I'm starving."

"Only if you pay," Lizzie said with a bright smile.

"Cheapskate. Fine, come on."

She laughed and took his hand, threading her arm through his as they walked with no particular destination in mind.

CHAPTER EIGHT

Rose threw the tennis ball, laughing as Callie sprinted in the opposite direction to fetch it. At the local dog park that evening—on her day off of work—she'd decided to get some much-needed fresh air to clear her head.

Callie returned with the ball and dropped it at Rose's feet. Rose ruffled the dog's fur. "Good girl," she crooned. "Go get it!"

She threw the ball so far that it landed in the lake. Not one to be put off by a little water, Callie jumped into the lake before Rose could catch her.

"Good thing I just had you groomed," Rose said in exasperation as Callie returned the ball. Callie panted, water dripping onto Rose's bare toes, and just waited for Rose to throw the ball for the millionth time.

Rose kept tossing the ball—far away from the lake each time—letting her mind drift.

She'd run into Seth a few times since she and Heath had returned from The Rise and Shine. Seth had been courteous but distant. Rose told herself it was for the best, although she couldn't help but resent her older brother a little. She knew Heath had said something to Seth, like she was still some little kid needing to be protected.

She grumbled under her breath. "Save me from overbearing men," she said to Callie as she threw the ball into the nearby woods. "I'd like to kick them all in the groin."

It was easier to think about Seth avoiding her like some kind of infectious disease than about Johnny's deadline creeping up on her. Her heart hammered in her chest each time she remembered that damn deadline.

*I almost have all the money*, she told herself. *If I can get him to just take the money…*

She wanted to believe she could persuade him to take the money and leave her alone. She wanted to believe it, even if her cynical side knew he wouldn't.

When she'd made her deal with Johnny, she hadn't realized all it would entail. She'd thought she'd live with him, maybe do chores for him. Cook him meals, make his bed, clean his house—things like that. She'd been so naïve.

Although she'd been almost twenty-one, she'd still been a virgin. Johnny had taken care of that quickly, though.

The old pain pushed up from her throat, making her eyes sting. She couldn't call it rape—not really.

She hadn't said no; yet she hadn't said yes, either.

She almost laughed at herself. If any other woman had told her a story like that, she would've called it rape within seconds. But it was easier to think she'd had a choice. It made it seem more bearable.

Johnny had never hurt her—not physically. He hadn't hit her; he hadn't bruised her. But he'd reminded her that she owed him, and that if she left, her brother would suffer the consequences. He'd reminded her that she would be nothing without him.

After a while, she'd believed him.

When Callie barked, Rose jumped, the present rushing back to her. The sun was about to set. How long had she been standing there, staring off into space?

As she walked toward the park's entrance, she realized that there were no other people or dogs around her. It wasn't that late—where was everyone? A little shiver chased down her spine, and she started walking more quickly. She felt for her gun, safely stowed in her jacket pocket like always.

Right then, some creature darted into the woods, Callie chasing after it with a loud bark. Rose shouted for her and was about to run after her dog when she heard a twig snap right behind her.

She didn't wait to see what it was: she whipped around and aimed her gun at whatever was following her. She waited, her body trembling with tension. She knew, with a certainty only gained by experience, that she was no longer alone.

"That's not very nice," Johnny said as he emerged from the woods like some creepy specter. "Pointing a gun at me."

Rose kept the gun leveled straight at his heart. "I still have time," she said in reply.

"I'm aware." He pulled out a packet of his stupid clove cigarettes, lighting one as he walked closer. He seemed completely unconcerned about the gun aimed straight at him. He took a drag of his cigarette, making Rose's eyes water from the smoke.

She hated the smell of cloves.

"I'd recommend you tell me what you want," she said.

Johnny laughed. "Would you believe me if I said I wanted to see you?"

"No."

"Too bad. I missed you. Did you miss me?" He blew out a cloud of smoke. "Then again, you have new friends. What's his name, Rosie?"

Her blood turned to ice. She gripped the gun harder, because she was afraid she'd drop it. Swallowing, she took a deep breath. "I don't know what you're talking about."

Even though the light was dim, she still saw the flash in Johnny's eyes. The same flash that signaled that he was no longer interested in playing nice. Stepping closer, he grabbed the gun's barrel so quickly that Rose gasped. Dropping his cigarette, he used his free hand to break her grip with a swift slice of his hand on her wrist. Before she knew it, she was disarmed, her gun tossed onto the trail, Johnny's arms wrapped around her in a grip like a boa constrictor and his forearm pushing against her throat.

"Who is he?" he asked again. "Do you think you can find someone else? You know what happens when you do that."

She gritted her teeth. When she'd first tried to escape Johnny, she'd enlisted one of his guys into helping her.

It had ended with his man getting beaten so badly as to be unrecognizable. He'd spent months in the hospital as a result.

The thought of Seth getting hurt like that—or worse—because of her terrified her. Seth was a soldier, but he had honor. He didn't know about the dirty tricks Johnny would play. And even a man like Seth couldn't defeat a bunch of guys intent on killing him.

"He's nobody. He's just my neighbor. Leave him out of this."

"A neighbor who kisses you? He's certainly dedicated to being neighborly."

He pushed his arm tighter against her throat until she saw stars. *God, he's been* watching *me. What else does he know?*

She clawed at his arm until he finally let up enough for her to breathe again. She gasped for air, but Johnny didn't let her go.

"I have your money," she rasped. "You said two weeks. I have three more days. Give me that, Johnny."

He seemed to consider her words. Right when it seemed like he was going to let her go, they both heard something running out of the woods. With a bark of warning, Callie launched herself at Johnny. He screamed, and Rose broke free. She saw the glint of her gun yards away; she said a prayer of thanks for whatever divine spirit had kept it from being lost in the woods.

"Get the fuck off of me!" Johnny yelled as Rose sprinted for her gun. She could hear cloth tearing, and she knew Callie had sunk her teeth into his leg with a force that was unbreakable.

Rose placed a hand on Callie's head to keep her still, although she didn't tell her to let Johnny go. "If you don't keep still, I'll tell her to rip out your throat," she said calmly as she pushed the barrel of the gun against the back of Johnny's neck.

He laughed, but she knew he was scared. *Good. Payback for all the times he terrified me.*

"Are you going to kill me?" he said lightly, although she almost smiled at the strain in his voice. Callie growled low in her throat.

"No, because I don't kill people. But unless you get the hell out of here and leave me alone, I'll rethink my decision."

Slowly, Johnny raised his hands in surrender. Rose commanded Callie to let him go, although she didn't move the gun from his neck. She wasn't about to let him try to hurt her dog.

"Walk. Now."

Johnny walked, swearing as he limped slowly. Rose could see the blood trail he left from his leg wound.

When they got to the entrance of the park, the sun having completely set and with no one in sight, Rose had him turn around.

"Get in your car, and drive. I don't care where. But get out of here."

He sneered. "That's it? You'll let me go?"

"Like I said: I will—for now."

He leaned toward her, but Callie gave a warning bark. He lurched away, his hands up.

"If you think this is over," he threatened, "you're wrong. We've just begun, Rosie." He swore at Callie as he limped to his car.

It wasn't until Johnny drove off that Rose put down her gun. And it was only minutes later—or was it hours? Days?—that she gasped and fell to her knees, the adrenaline rushing away to be replaced by stark fear.

She clutched Callie tightly. "What am I going to do?" she whispered.

No one answered.

~

Rose didn't expect to sleep that night. She kept her gun close as she curled up in her nest of blankets on the floor, Callie only feet away. When Callie wouldn't stop pacing, however, Rose gave in and let Callie join her in her "bed."

"Just for this once," she whispered. She knew full well she was doing it more for herself than for Callie.

Callie's warm weight and the quiet sounds of the night lulled Rose to sleep, but not before her thoughts turned toward Seth. She wondered if she should tell him what was going on. Didn't he have a right to know, now that Johnny had threatened to hurt him?

She knew the answer. He deserved to know, even if it humiliated her. And even if he never looked at her the same way again.

That thought was her last as she fell asleep. Her dreams were scattered, bizarre, more colors and shapes and sounds than anything else. She vaguely remembered waking up and feeling Callie's nose next to her ear. But perhaps she'd dreamed it.

Then her dreams became distinctly erotic.

She was—in a cabin? In her apartment?—at the moment, it didn't matter, because this was a dream. She wore only a lacy negligee, her hair falling down around her shoulders. Roses scented the air; candles were lit throughout. She sat on a bed and waited. She already knew who she waited for, and her heart pounded with anticipation.

Seth entered the room and gave her a heated once-over. Every place his gaze touched felt like fireworks exploding beneath her skin. She rose and pressed her hands against his hard chest—blessedly, wonderfully bare—and she felt the rumble of his voice before she heard it.

"Rose." He leaned down to kiss the soft spot beneath her ear. "I want you."

Those simple words nearly made her knees buckle. Sweeping her off her feet, he carried her to the bed and laid her down on the duvet covered in rose petals that had appeared. And then she was naked, and so was he, and she explored him like she'd wanted to do since she'd first met him. She explored him with a courage she didn't have outside of dreams.

In dreams, she could be the woman she ached to be.

She didn't know what he looked like under his clothes, but her imagination was vivid regardless. His chest was sprinkled with dark hair, and she traced the lines of his abdomen. He was all muscles and strength and heat, and he smelled like pure male.

He tangled his fingers in her hair and pulled her up for a kiss that shattered her senses. She felt his body press against her own, so hard against her softness, and she shivered when his cock brushed her hip.

He kissed her until time seemed to stop. He kissed her neck, her breasts, laving her straining nipples. She felt wetness pool between her legs.

"Seth, please. Seth."

He kissed her belly. He muttered her name. But when he looked up, he was no longer Seth.

It was Johnny.

"I'm so glad you came back to me, Rosie," he crooned, caressing her hip. "Because you've always been mine."

And she screamed.

∼

She awoke to the sound of her own screaming. It seemed to go on and on. She clapped a hand over her mouth, but sounds still leaked through. Callie barked; Rose shushed her.

She couldn't stop trembling. All she could see was Johnny's eyes, his smile, the way he knew he had her and always would. Feeling sick, she rose from the tangled mess of her blankets to stumble to the bathroom. After throwing up the little bit that was in her stomach, she washed out her mouth and brushed her teeth for good measure. Callie followed her around the entire time in canine concern.

When she heard the knock on her front door, she jumped. Callie barked. Her heart pounding furiously, she grabbed her gun from next to her pillow and went to the door. And waited.

Another knock. Then: "Rose, it's Seth. Let me in. I heard you scream."

He said the words softly, but she heard the command under them. If she weren't so freaked out, she'd be annoyed by his tone. She considered telling him to go away, but did she want to be alone right now?

No, she really, really didn't.

She opened the door to see Seth wearing only boxers, his hair mussed from sleep. Her breath caught. Although it was obviously dark, the illumination from the streetlamps let her know her imagination hadn't been far off the mark. If anything, her imagination hadn't been generous enough.

He was cut as if from marble, from his chest to his abdomen. Her gaze traced the line of his hip to the waistband of his boxers.

He cleared his throat, and she jumped.

"Can I come in?" He looked at the gun still in her hand. "Or are you going to really shoot me this time?"

"Oh. Oh, no. Come in." She gestured for him to follow her, all too aware she herself wore nothing but a tank top and sleep shorts—and no bra. Nobody sane wore a bra to bed, but at the moment, she rather wished she'd kept hers on, because her nipples were already hardening with sheer want.

She set the gun on the kitchen counter and then turned on a lamp in the living room. She blinked at the wash of light, a headache beginning to pound in her temples.

"You heard me?" she asked quietly, suddenly embarrassed. Her cheeks heated, and then they heated even more when she couldn't offer Seth a place to sit. She just had her single chair in the living room.

"Heard you screaming? Anyone would've heard that. Be glad the couple on the other side of you is out of town, other-wise they probably would've called the cops." He eyed her with concern.

She massaged her temples. "It was just a dream. A bad one. I'm sorry to have woken you up."

"I was already awake." And then with a twisted smile that made her heart ache, he added, "I have nightmares, too."

It was strange, this bizarre camaraderie now forming between them. What horrors haunted Seth? No wonder he had dark circles under his eyes so many mornings.

"You can sit, if you like," she offered.

"And you can sit on the floor?" He shook his head before sitting on the floor in front of the chair. He patted the chair.

She finally sat down, pulling her legs under her. Callie stood guard next to her.

Even though he was below her, wearing only boxers, and obviously exhausted, Seth still managed to seem commanding.

His dark eyes assessed her, and she had to restrain herself from looking away.

That gaze could strip her bare within moments—figuratively and literally.

"So," he said quietly, his gaze never wavering, "are you going to finally tell me what's going on?"

# CHAPTER NINE

Seth watched as a shudder fell across Rose's features, and it only made him want to know her better. Shouldn't women burst into tears and tell men like him about all the monsters under the bed?

He almost snorted. He'd never met a woman like that and he probably never would. He only dealt with stubborn women, brave women, *annoying* women. Like his twin, Lizzie.

"I don't want to talk about it," Rose finally said.

He clucked his tongue. "Look, I heard you screaming. Screaming, Rose. Something's going on, and I'm not leaving this apartment until you tell me what it is."

Anger flashed in her eyes. Good. He could deal with anger better than he could deal with hysterics. He understood anger.

She glared down at him from her perch on her chair. "I didn't think you were into harassment, Seth Thornton."

"I'm not, but I know when somebody needs to talk. You need to talk. You look like shit, by the way."

That made her laugh, which he'd hoped it would. "You're an asshole. Go away."

Before he thought about the consequences, he reached up and pulled her down onto the floor to sit beside him. Her eyes widened, but she didn't protest. She was warm and soft and smelled like flowers, and he almost buried his nose in the crook of her neck. When she sat halfway on his lap, her hands on his shoulders, she seemed like she wasn't sure if she wanted to leave his embrace.

Then Callie sneezed, and Rose scrambled away from him.

"Why do you have a gun?" he prodded again. "What scares you? Or who?"

"Maybe I'm just paranoid."

"Don't deflect."

She sighed. She tugged at her braid, which had loosened during sleep. He forced himself not to think about Rose in bed —in *his* bed—soft and sleepy and a temptation like no other.

"I have nightmares, too," he repeated.

She stilled, but she didn't say anything.

"My last tour in Afghanistan…we were on a convoy trip. Nothing but standard procedure. We were just a few miles from base, and we hadn't had any trouble. Max and I were going to play ball that evening. I'd won our last match and he wanted to even the score."

Seth swallowed against the lump in his throat. "We'd done three tours together. He'd been a pain in the ass the entire time. When we first met, he told me I couldn't sit around brooding and that he'd make me laugh at something stupid. I held out for a while, but then he told this joke about a fucking toucan and I laughed. After that…"

He closed his eyes, seeing Max's wide smile, the way he tipped his head back when he laughed. Max had been carefree, and everyone had loved him. He was one of those people other people gravitated toward. When Seth had joined the Marines, he'd been lost, needing purpose; Lizzie had run off, and his parents had disapproved of his wandering ways. He'd lost touch with any friends from high school.

Max had been there, though. And when Max had asked Seth to be his daughter's godfather, he'd said yes without hesitation.

"One second we were joking, shooting the shit. The next —an explosion so loud that I thought I'd gone permanently deaf. It's like being thrown by a tornado or something. You can't fight it; you just have to hope you land without being broken in two."

Rose had moved closer to him and placed a hand on his knee. "Seth, I'm so sorry."

He shook his head. "Don't apologize to me. Apologize to Max's wife, Jessica, and to their baby girl. I couldn't save him. It should've been me, not him."

He'd never said that thought out loud. Rose's breath caught, and her hand gripped his knee. Then she took his hand and squeezed.

He allowed the touch for a moment until he gently pulled away. "That's what my nightmares are about." He shrugged, because what else could he do? Cry? Yell? Scream? It was what it was. Life was shitty more often than not and you just had to push through it.

"I've heard you. During the night," she admitted. Her cheeks turned a little pink. "And you know what I thought?"

"What?"

"I was glad I wasn't the only one. How terrible is that?" She tugged on her braid, the blue tips bright against her pale skin. "I'm so glad someone else is suffering, too." She shook her head.

"That's not terrible." At her continued head-shaking, he said more firmly, "It isn't. It's just…human."

"So we're both human?" She smiled sadly. "How sad. How mortal."

She had yet to tell him what was going on with her, but he could wait. In this instance, he'd wait until the end of time for her. He didn't want to consider why—why now, why this woman—but there it was.

She kept pulling at her hair until it was about to come out of its braid. "If I tell you what's going on, will you promise not to tell anyone? And I mean *anyone.* Not the police, not your brothers, nobody."

After a long moment, he nodded.

"I already told you that my ex won't leave me alone. There's more to it than that."

His lips twisted. "I figured."

In halting tones, she told him about how she'd met Johnny Porter at college. How she'd fallen for him quickly, how he'd seemed so charming and thoughtful and smart. How she'd been sheltered from the world thanks to Heath, and although she didn't blame her brother at all, she wished she hadn't been so naïve. So innocent.

"This part, you can't tell anyone. Promise me." Her face was pale and drawn.

He took her hand and squeezed it. "I promise, Rose."

She told him of Heath's arrest, of the drugs. How she'd known Heath was innocent, but he hadn't had any money to get a good lawyer. How Johnny had told her he'd get the charges dropped and erased, and how she'd agreed to whatever Johnny had wanted.

With every word, Seth's anger increased. He wanted to find that weasel of an ex-boyfriend and beat him until he sobbed for mercy. His hands twitched in his lap, and he could feel a vein pulsing in his forehead.

"But mostly I'm telling you this because I'm afraid for you," she said quickly.

He blinked. "*Me?*"

"Johnny, he's—he's seen us. Together." She swallowed. "He found me at the park today and threatened not only me, but you. I knew you should know. If you should be hurt because of me…" That finally caused her to sob, but she looked away.

"Rose, princess, look at me." She wouldn't look at him; she just shook her head. "I can take care of myself. And if that piece of shit gets near you again, I'll kill him."

That made her look up. "No, you can't. Please. He has friends, people who can hurt you and your family. Don't do anything stupid. Promise me."

"You've been asking me to promise a lot tonight."

"I just wanted to warn you. I almost have the money, and this will be over. I swear it."

She became so agitated that she started trembling. He hauled her into his arms, the top of her head tucked under his chin. She shivered like she'd been caught in the snow, and he rubbed her arms and murmured sweet nothings in her ear.

He stroked her hair until she calmed, but he didn't let her go. He couldn't.

"I'm not going to let anything happen to you," he vowed. "If I promise anything, it's that."

"Oh, Seth…"

"Don't tell me no. Don't tell me you'll take care of your-self. I'm a soldier; I can take care of myself and I can take care of you." When she looked up at him, he touched her cheek with a gentle caress. "I'll watch over you, Rose."

Her bottom lip trembled, and she buried her face in his shoulder. She didn't cry; she just clung to him until her terror came under control.

To his surprise, she didn't tell him to go home or move away. She tilted her head back, and looking at him from under her lashes, she whispered, "Kiss me, Seth. Make me forget."

THE DECISION HAD BEEN INSTANTANEOUS, but it felt right. Rose thought of her dream that had been polluted with Johnny near the end. She wanted that nightmare eradicated by reality. Here in Seth's arms, she felt safer than she'd felt in a long time.

When he vowed to keep her safe, she believed him.

His eyes darkened, his pupils expanding until there was barely any iris left. She ached for his kiss like she'd never ached for anything in her life. Although her nightmares and her memories were present, she could push them aside right now.

She wanted something *good*. Something bright and clean and lovely. She wanted to be wanted for herself for once.

"Kiss me," she said again. She pressed her hand against his thumping heart, and she felt him inhale.

When she felt his cock harden under her, she knew he wanted her as much as she wanted him.

"I'm not going to take advantage of you," he said, but he didn't sound convinced. His eye twitched; his jaw was clenched.

She trailed her fingers along his hard jaw, feeling the stubble there. "You're not taking advantage if I want it."

"You're tired. You should sleep."

She bit back a smile. Rising up, she looped her arms around his neck. "I'm not tired. And I don't want to sleep right now."

When she kissed him, she almost lost her courage when he didn't move. He was like a statue in her arms—albeit a warm one. One who smelled so good and was so handsome it made her heart flutter every time she saw him.

She broke the kiss and stared into his eyes. She waited.

Then, he wrapped her in his arms and muttered a curse under his breath before he kissed her.

He didn't just kiss her—he *enveloped* her.

Rose moaned, long and low, as his kiss deepened. She thought of their kiss outside, and she could say easily that that one couldn't compare. This one made her skin feel too tight for her body, and she longed to have his fingers brush every inch of her. She opened her mouth further, making the kiss even more intense, but he laughed under his breath.

"Patience," he soothed, his hands coasting down her spine. "We have all night."

He didn't understand—they didn't have all night. They only had this moment. She began to kiss down his neck, licking at the salty taste she found there, and he tugged at her braid.

She found herself lifted into his arms a second later, and he carried her to her bedroom. She wasn't even embarrassed that she didn't have a bed: just a nest of blankets and pillows. It was a far cry from her dream, that was for sure, but this was better. In a dream, you couldn't feel a man's heat, or feel the play of his muscles. You couldn't smell him, or discover scars and moles and freckles that marked him as painfully human.

Rose traced a scar on his left pectoral right as he laid her down in her nest. Callie had followed them and stood near the door, which made Rose laugh. Seth frowned and then looked over his shoulder.

"Callie, go lie down," Rose said. Callie hesitated before trotting to her bed; Rose could hear her huffing out a sad doggy sigh at being banished.

With the moonlight coming through the window, it bathed Seth in an ethereal light. Rose almost wondered if this were another dream. Yet as Seth pushed her tank up to expose her belly, she knew this was truly happening.

After Johnny, Rose hadn't wanted any man to touch her. She hadn't dated, and she definitely hadn't slept with anyone. It had been too painful, and it had only reminded her of what Johnny had destroyed.

Tonight, though, she wanted a man for the first time in years. It thrilled her as much as it scared her.

Seth kissed her, caressing her, not pushing her to go any faster. His lips were surprisingly soft for a man who presented such a tough exterior. What other secrets did Seth Thornton's heart hold? She wanted to know all of them: the good, the bad, and even the ugly.

"You're so beautiful," he said as he kissed down her neck. He pulled her hair tie from her braid and fanned the locks over her shoulder. "Why the blue?"

"I wanted something different." She shrugged. "I didn't want to be like anybody else."

"No one would think that of you."

Her heart beat faster; she had to close her eyes for a moment to reorient herself. It didn't help that Seth continued to kiss her and caress her, his fingers so gentle she wanted to cry.

"We don't have to do anything tonight," he said again.

Her eyes flew open. The thought of him leaving—she clutched at him. "No, no. I want you to stay. I want *you*."

She pulled off her tank top and was about to take off her pajama shorts when Seth stopped her.

"Like I said: we have time. Don't rush this."

She nodded, and then when she saw the heat in his eyes as he gazed at her bare breasts, she felt like flames were licking across her skin.

Her breasts were on the small side, and she didn't have to wear a bra all the time if she didn't want to. Johnny had always hated her small breasts, telling her he'd pay for implants, but she'd never accepted his oh-so-generous offer.

Right then, she was glad she hadn't.

"Beautiful," Seth breathed as he brushed his thumb across one straining nipple.

Rose was sitting up, but at his touch on her breast, she fell back onto her blankets. Rising over her, Seth took her breast into his mouth, the feeling so shocking that all the air left her lungs.

She arched, she moaned, she begged. He sucked one nipple and rolled the other, and she'd never known her breasts could be this sensitive. Running her fingers through his hair, she whispered his name like a benediction.

As he kissed her breasts, she managed to push her pajama shorts and panties to her ankles. Seth's gaze met hers when he felt her bare hip brush his own.

"Touch me," she breathed. "Please."

He sent her a wicked grin, and when he began to lick at one nipple while his hand found her swollen sex, she bit her lip to keep from screaming. Or maybe from crying. She wasn't sure anymore.

He parted her, growling when he touched her there, and she could feel herself growing wetter with every stroke. She bucked against his searching hand, but he refused to give her the release she so desperately wanted. Not yet.

"Widen your legs for me. That's it, princess. I can feel how much you want me and it's driving me insane." He stared down at her now, his fingers spreading her wetness, delving into her tight sheath ever so slightly.

She clutched his biceps. "Don't call me that," she managed to squeak out.

He laughed. "You're right. You know what I thought you were after that second time I met you?"

She wanted to die; she wanted to kick him. When he began to rub her clit in slow circles, she started gasping.

"I thought, 'She's not a princess. She's a hummingbird. All color and movement.'" He started rubbing faster, his index finger pressing inside her.

Stuffing her fist into her mouth, Rose wondered if you could die from wanting. And right as her release hit her, she experienced not only the untold pleasure from Seth's skilled fingers, but a fear that had been lurking in the corners of her mind all night.

She struggled to find herself within the shadows even as

her orgasm made her cry out. She wanted to hold Seth close and push him away. As she opened her eyes, the moon had moved so it was too dark to see Seth's face. Was it still him? Or was this another version of her nightmare?

But then he kissed her, and she tasted him on her lips. She wrapped her arms and legs around him, and he laughed again.

"Hummingbird, what are you—? No, it's all right. I'm here. Hush."

She struggled to keep herself from sobbing. She was so mixed up, so confused. Why had she done this? She was so stupid. She needed to think.

She needed to be alone.

When she managed to find her equilibrium again, her body no longer trembling from her release, she rose from the nest of blankets.

She could just make out Seth frowning up at her.

"What is it?" he asked. "Are you okay?"

She almost shook her head, then stopped. "I need to go to sleep," was the only response she could muster.

The clouds covering the moon moved again, and she saw his confusion. His hurt. Her heart twisted. Then he rose and kissed her—hard—before leaving her to be alone again.

Just like she wanted.

CHAPTER TEN

The weekend before the Fourth of July, the entire Thornton clan and their various significant others rented a boat to celebrate Caleb's thirty-fourth birthday. Caleb had told Megan he didn't want anything big, but she'd decided that he should definitely have a party. Not only to celebrate his birthday, but to celebrate his promotion at work.

When Caleb and Megan got on the boat, everyone yelled "Surprise!" when they walked to the stern. Caleb jumped a little and then laughed.

"Happy birthday!" Megan kissed him with a smacking sound, and Seth was amused to notice his brother blushing a little.

"Didn't I tell you I didn't want a party?" Caleb shook his head, but he looked pleased nonetheless. "How did you manage to plan this without me knowing?"

"Oh, a woman never tells her secrets," Megan demurred.

That resulted in laughter all around, and then the drinks were being poured. Since Harrison had rented the boat, they had a captain to make certain the boat didn't go anywhere it shouldn't, which really just meant everyone could drink to their heart's content.

Seth grabbed a beer from the cooler and watched his siblings—Harrison with his wife, Sara; Caleb with his wife, Megan; Mark with his wife, Abby; Lizzie with Trent (and Bea, as she couldn't be away from Lizzie very long), and then Jubilee. Megan had also invited Trent's brother, Ash, and his sister, Thea; and then, to Seth's utter delight, there was Heath DiMarco, glaring at him from the top deck.

Seth had heard someone mention Rose's name and that she'd been invited, but she'd apparently declined to attend.

Of course she had. He drank his beer with quick gulps.

Lizzie, with Bea in a front pack, came over to Seth and looked up. Then she whistled.

"Did you kill his dog?" she asked semiseriously. "Oh, wait —is this about Rose?"

Seth didn't answer.

He hadn't seen Rose in days following their night together, only hearing her door open and close when she arrived home. They'd briefly run into each other yesterday, but she'd stuttered something random and hurried away. He'd been this close to pulling her into his apartment and demanding answers.

After their night together, he'd thought—what? That they'd make things official? He didn't know what their relationship even was. He did know, however, that he would keep her safe no matter what she said or did. His blood boiled at the mere memory of what that asshole Johnny had done to her.

"It's complicated," Seth finally replied when Heath turned away to talk to Harrison.

"Hmm, isn't it always?" Lizzie crooned to Bea, "Your uncle Seth is so mysterious, isn't he? I bet he'd tell his favorite niece all his secrets."

Seth smiled. Looking at Bea's bright blue eyes and toothless smile, he definitely couldn't deny that assertion. He'd do anything for this little girl. She had everyone wrapped around her tiny pinky.

"Here, can you hold her? I need to go to the bathroom." Lizzie handed him Bea with a bright smile before he could protest.

Not that he'd say no. In the passing weeks since Bea's birth—she was three months old now, wasn't she?—he'd gotten more comfortable around her. She was an easy baby to like, though. Lizzie had been shocked when not only did Bea sleep through the night most nights, but she was only fussy when she was hungry or tired or wet. The usual kinds of reasons to fuss.

Right now, Bea reached up to grab Seth's nose. Her fingers were wet and she smelled like baby powder, but Seth's heart did that annoying twist that it always did when he held his niece.

Who knew someone so small could affect your life so profoundly?

"What do you think I should do?" he murmured to Bea as he took her to look out over the stern. The lake was bright and shining, and it was a perfect day for boating. Seagulls flew about, cawing, and he watched as one flew down to catch a fish near the surface of the water. Seth pulled Bea's sun hat further down so the sun wouldn't hurt her eyes. Should she wear sunglasses? Did babies wear sunglasses?

Bea didn't have an answer for him, but just cooed and squealed when another seagull dove into the water.

"I think she's running from me, but I don't know why," he said. "It's like she tells me one thing and does another." He sighed, long and low. "Any other woman, I'd assume she was playing games and would move on."

He said that, yet he knew Rose wasn't like other women. He knew this wasn't some game with her, but did he have the patience—and the ability—to overcome whatever was haunting her?

Seth was certain there was more to her story with Johnny than she'd let on. All kinds of horrible things had wandered into his mind, and by the time the sun had risen after he'd returned to his apartment the night they'd been together, he'd been close to wanting to find Johnny and kill him himself.

"Do you think I should keep trying? Not give up on her?"

Bea patted his cheek, gurgling some nonsense, but Seth took that as a yes.

*You're not going to be rid of me that easily, hummingbird. I swear it.*

"I'm back. Oh goodness, what a happy baby you are." Lizzie held out her arms for Bea, and Seth gave her back a little reluctantly. "What were you two talking about?"

"Nothing you need to hear about."

She rolled her eyes. "Try again. Otherwise I'm going to follow you around throughout this entire party until you spill."

Seth considered. He wasn't about to tell Lizzie about Rose, but he hadn't mentioned Sergeant Loyd calling him and about his offer. In all honesty, he'd barely thought about returning to active duty with everything happening with Rose lately.

"My CO called me," he said. He watched Lizzie's face,

but his twin sister didn't betray any agitation at this pronouncement.

"What did he want? Something paperwork-related?"

Seth ran his fingers through his hair. "No, not exactly. He has a job for me."

"A job. For you."

"He wants me for a mission that's coming up, and he said if I agree, he can get me back on active duty by the fall."

Lizzie's eyes widened. "Seth, are you serious? When did he call and tell you this?"

"Um, two weeks ago?"

"Seth!"

"I know, I know. I've had a lot on my mind." It was a lame excuse, but there it was.

He winced as he saw the hurt on Lizzie's face. They'd always told each other everything, and although they'd drifted apart, he knew she'd hoped they could return to how they used to be. She'd told him all about her troubles with Trent and her music career, yet he hadn't had the courage to reciprocate.

"I'm sorry I didn't tell you. Really. I just don't know how to answer."

"Say no!" She touched his arm and said more quietly, "That last mission almost killed you. You lost your best friend. What happens if this tour ends up being your last?"

He had thought the same, but he didn't want to admit it. Patting her hand, he said, "It won't be, Lizard. I haven't given Sergeant Loyd an answer yet, either."

That didn't seem to console her. In fact, it made her expression even sadder. "You're going to take it, aren't you?"

*No. I don't know. Maybe. What am I if I'm not a soldier?* He struggled to explain, but right then, Caleb came up to them with three beers in hand.

"Hey, what are you two doing? Lizzie, you can drink, and Seth, you can *definitely* drink. It's my birfday! No, birthday. Hmm, drinking." He took a slug of beer and wandered off to bug some other people.

That interlude broke the tension, and Lizzie and Seth laughed. Then with a conspiratorial smile, Lizzie whispered, "Did you notice that Sara isn't drinking?"

"No, why would I?"

"You're such a guy. *Think.* You think she's pregnant?"

The last thing Seth had ever considered was whether or not one of his brothers' wives was pregnant, but it wouldn't surprise him. The Thorntons enjoyed their spouses; ergo, babies would inevitably result.

"Harrison does seem extra happy lately," Lizzie mused.

Seth frowned. "Really?"

"Oh my God! Yes! Come on, Seth, pay attention."

"I am," he mumbled before finishing off his beer.

"I'm surprised she hasn't said anything. Maybe they're waiting."

"Lizard, why in God's name would I know anything about it?"

Both she and Bea gave him disgusted looks, although Bea's might have just been from gas.

"I'm going to go talk to Megan and see if she knows anything. Go make sure Caleb doesn't fall overboard."

The party continued through the afternoon: Caleb declared his love for Megan in front of everyone (to both her delight and her embarrassment) and then proceeded to seduce her. She then ran away, with him stumbling after her.

Harrison and Sara didn't drink at all, which made Seth think Lizzie's supposition was correct. Harrison was probably abstaining out of solidarity—or because Sara had told him that was his payment for her being the one to give birth.

Even Mark got a little tipsy, which resulted in him and Abby laughing together in some corner like a couple of teenagers. Seth couldn't believe the change in Mark since Seth had returned from overseas. Where had his brusque older brother gone? Clearly Abby had done something miraculous to get him out of his shell. Seth had thought for a long time that Mark only loved his horses. At least now he loved his horses *and* Abby.

Trent carried Bea around so Lizzie could have a break, and Trent's siblings, Ash and Thea, took turns holding their niece. Bea loved people, and she didn't mind being held by just about anything human. *That girl's going to break hearts*, Seth mused as he watched Ash fall in love with Bea even further when she grabbed his chin.

One person, however, made a point to avoid Seth entirely: Heath. And considering that Seth didn't feel like having a rehash of their issues with each other, Seth avoided Heath as well. They circled each other like wild dogs throughout the party, and even Caleb—as drunk as he was—noticed the burning stares the two men gave each other.

"Seth! Seth, Seth, Seth," Caleb said as he slung an arm over Seth's shoulder, making Caleb's glass of liquor slosh onto the deck. "I love you, bro. I'm glad you're back. You should come over more." Caleb started patting Seth's face like Bea would, and Seth pushed him away.

"Caleb, you idiot—"

"No, I'm not. You are. You're so stupid." Caleb finished

off his drink. "Don't make the same mistakes I did. I almost lost the woman I loved—for what? Pride?" He snorted. "Not worth it, believe me."

Seth froze. How the hell did Caleb know anything…? Seth narrowed his eyes when he spotted Lizzie. She caught his look and shrugged.

His damn siblings and their big mouths.

"I won't be stupid like you because I never am," Seth quipped. "Now, how about I get you some water before you start throwing up over the side of the boat?"

Megan took charge of her husband right then and got him to drink a bottle of water, giggling when he yanked her into his lap for a loud kiss.

The evening ended when Harrison called for a toast. "I'm glad we could all get together tonight," he said. "Caleb, happy birthday, man. You've come a long way in the last year."

Caleb's eyes shimmered, making Seth look away. He knew Caleb had his own secrets, which Seth had only found out about upon returning to Fair Haven; it had taken a lot of courage—and Megan's love—for Caleb to come to grips with a teenage tragedy he'd caused.

Harrison's words sobered Caleb instantly; he drank his bottle of water in silence with Megan on his lap. She murmured something in his ear, which caused him to sigh and lean against her shoulder.

"Caleb hasn't drunk any booze since he got with Megan," Lizzie whispered in Seth's ear. "She told him to have fun tonight, but…"

Ah. Seth put the pieces together and suddenly wished he could give his older brother a big hug. "He should enjoy himself. He deserves it."

"He does." She clinked glasses with Seth. "And so do you, just FYI."

Harrison raised his glass again, and everyone went quiet. "One more thing—and Sara has given me permission to say this." He looked down at his wife and squeezed her hand, the love between them palpable. "Sara and I are pregnant. Due in February."

That resulted in a lot of squealing and yelling, and then Harrison and Sara were enveloped in so many hugs that they disappeared from Seth's line of sight for a moment. Lizzie yanked on Seth's arm, saying that she knew Sara was pregnant, and then Seth finally managed to find Harrison and give him a hug.

"Congrats," Seth said in all sincerity.

"Thanks. We're excited." Harrison's eyes gleamed. "I'm glad you'll be here for the birth, too."

Guilt swamped him, because Seth could very well be abroad again, but he didn't say that. Smiling tightly, he congratulated Sara and passed the rest of the evening watching his family enjoy themselves while his own thoughts were back in Fair Haven with a woman he couldn't get out of his head.

# CHAPTER ELEVEN

When Rose heard Seth cry out in the middle of the night, her heart twisted. It wasn't a shout like when you stubbed a toe or banged your knee against a piece of furniture: it was the kind of cry that was equal parts terror and rage. It was the kind of shout that she understood all too well.

She closed her eyes and dug her fingers into Callie's plush fur. She waited for another shout, but there was only silence from next door.

Rose hadn't been able to sleep, although Seth's yell would've awoken her, no doubt. Rising from her blankets, she padded to the living room, which shared a wall with Seth's apartment.

She placed her ear against the wall and listened. She could make out Seth walking around, and she heard his low voice. It was too muffled to hear his words, but it confirmed that he was awake.

Callie stood next to her and woofed softly. Rose petted her absently.

She'd missed him—that she couldn't deny. She'd avoided him since she'd essentially kicked him out of her apartment, but she'd listened for him to come home every day. The evenings she had to leave for work before he had returned had been the hardest. When she heard him walking around his apartment, or heard the TV switch on, or heard him banging on she didn't even know what, it was soothing.

It meant that Johnny hadn't enacted his plan to hurt Seth.

She shuddered. Tendrils of fear curled around her heart.

Then she heard Seth groan, and if his shout had made her heart twist, this groan made her long to embrace him. She wanted to take away all his hurts.

"Go lie down," she told Callie as she grabbed her keys. She didn't stop to think about what she was doing. If she did, she knew she'd stay in her apartment for the rest of the night.

Rose knocked on Seth's door, and when he opened it, she almost jumped. He looked pale and exhausted, with dark circles under his eyes. But she was mostly surprised by the fierceness in his expression. It took him a moment to register who was standing in front of him.

"Rose? What are you doing here?"

She struggled against a flood of embarrassment. *What am I doing here? Excellent question.*

"I heard you. I wanted to make sure you were okay."

His jaw clenched, and Rose almost wondered if he would tell her to go away. She'd never seen him so ill at ease: Seth had always seemed so capable, so put-together. Right now, though, he seemed vulnerable and all-too-human.

"Come in, then. Before you freeze." He gestured for her to enter, and Rose realized with a start that this was the first time she'd seen his apartment. He'd always come over to her place.

It was almost amusing, seeing the mirror version of her place with actual furniture in it. There were some pictures on the wall, including photos of baby Bea. But Rose instantly found herself wandering toward a section of the living room that had become a sort-of workstation.

It was filled with wood, and Rose marveled at a table that was being created. She discovered a few smaller pieces set on a table: a carved horse, a guitar. When she picked up a carved bird, she heard Seth inhale a breath.

Her eyes widened when she realized it was a humming-bird. *You're like a hummingbird: all color and movement.*

Stroking the smooth lines of the bird's wings, she felt the walls around her heart collapsing. Why did this man have to be so frustrating and wonderful at the same time?

She set the hummingbird down before turning toward Seth. He'd been watching her with an assessing look, like he couldn't make her out. Well, he wasn't alone, she thought. She could barely make herself out lately.

"Do you want to talk about it? Your nightmare?" She took his hand and entwined her fingers with his.

"Not really. I want to talk about why you're here when you've been avoiding me all week."

She dropped his hand, and he gave her a wry look. Opening her mouth to explain, she found herself unable to explain her actions. And the thought of telling him of what Johnny had done to her…

"I just freaked out. I'm sorry. I didn't handle it well."

He sighed. "Why are you here, Rose?"

It was funny: she'd asked him if he'd wanted to talk, but she suddenly wanted to do everything *but* talk. Words seemed futile at this point. Instead, she drank him in: from his dark eyes, to the stubble on his cheeks, to the dark hair bisecting his abdomen. She was infinitely grateful for his disinterest in shirts. He should never wear a shirt: it was a crime against humanity that he covered up that magnificent body of his.

Her body was buzzing, like it had filled with an electric current. She bit her lip, torn between physical desire and emotional fear, and Seth saw the gesture with his hawk-like gaze. He narrowed his eyes as he looked at her mouth for a long, heated moment.

Shivering, she looked away, effectively breaking the moment. "How long have you been doing this?" She gestured at the table, the figurines. "You've never mentioned it."

She saw him shrug in her peripheral vision. "I learned how to do it in high school, but I've only taken it up again recently. I work part-time at Alan's shop."

"Of course you just took up woodworking again and are this good at it." She shook her head. She knew next to nothing about how to shape wood into tables and chairs and hummingbirds, but she could recognize skill when she saw it. "This is amazing," she said truthfully as she once again picked up the hummingbird.

"I like to do smaller works to get my mind off things. The horse is kind of messed up—its head is too big."

She hadn't noticed, but now that she looked at the horse, it did seem rather out of proportion. The hummingbird, however, was perfect—almost. She realized that one wing was slightly bigger than the other, but oddly enough, it made it even more precious to her.

It made the maker seem more human, and she marveled at how lifelike the figurine seemed regardless. He'd even carved the individual feathers on its body and wings.

"You can have that," he said. At her surprised look, he laughed a little. "I think I carved it with you in mind, you know."

She brushed a finger down the bird's neck. Closing her eyes, she thought, *Don't break my heart, Seth. Because you could, so easily.*

"You never answered my question: why are you here, Rose?"

She set the hummingbird down a second time. But when she turned toward Seth, she said, "I want to touch you like you touched me."

SETH WAS sure he hadn't heard her correctly. Gazing up at him from under her lashes, she had a slight flush to her cheeks and he could see that her nipples were peaked under her tank top. He swallowed, a lump in his throat.

He'd get whiplash from how many times Rose changed her mind, but right in that moment, with his cock so hard it ached, he didn't care. He didn't care if she kicked him out of his apartment afterward.

To touch her—to have her touch *him*—it would be worth it.

He took her hand and pressed it right over his pounding heart. "If you think I'm going to stop you," he rasped, "you're crazy."

She shot him a quick grin, but it turned into a sigh of pleasure as she caressed his chest before tracing a line down to his belly button. His abdomen tensed.

With only his boxers covering his erection, she had to

know how much he wanted her. Yet she didn't seem in a hurry: something his mind appreciated but his body wanted to protest. He needed her hands on his cock—and God, her mouth. He shuddered at the mere thought of something so divine.

Rose was tentative, but not fearful. Yet he sensed that she was inexperienced, like when she brushed her thumb over one of his nipples and frowned when he didn't erupt into loud moans like she had. He bit his lip to keep from laughing, although the furrow in her brow was so adorable he wanted to kiss it away.

"I love your body," she said on a heartfelt sigh. "When you came to my door that first time without your shirt on…"

"Had a few dirty thoughts, hummingbird?"

"You could say that." Her grin this time was impish. "If I told you that I touched myself the next night thinking of you, what would you say to that?"

He groaned and said a prayer to some deity to help him, save him. She was going to kill him.

"I'd say that you're going to drive me absolutely insane."

"Good. I like seeing you lose control."

Seth gritted his teeth as her breasts brushed against his chest, and he gritted them even harder when she kissed him between his collarbone. Her hot little tongue laved his skin. He gripped her waist, more so to hold himself steady than to keep her upright.

"How about we move this to the bedroom?" he suggested.

"No, I like it here." Right then, she kneeled in front of him, and he almost came out of his skin. "Don't move, Thornton."

As if he would move. He'd stand right here until the end of the time if she asked him to.

Rose hesitated—it was only a split second, but it made alarm bells go off in his brain. She'd essentially kicked him out of her place after their last encounter, and now he wondered if she was pushing herself too hard, too fast.

"Rose, you don't have to do anything tonight. It's fine."

That only made her eyes flash. He should've known saying something like that would dare her not to give up on what she'd intended to do. Well, he might very well get burned, but was it worth it?

When Rose slowly pulled his boxers down to reveal his cock, he knew the answer: absolutely fucking worth it.

He'd never been this hard for a woman. He clenched his fists to keep himself from touching her. Because if he touched her, he'd carry her straight to his bedroom and be inside her in five seconds flat.

"You're huge," she said with wide eyes, and her expression almost made him laugh again. And, yes, it also made his head swell—he was a guy, he couldn't help it.

She looked up at him again, licking her lips. "Tell me what you like. What I should do."

He tanged his fingers in her hair, but he didn't press her. He knew that although he was receiving pleasure, this was almost more about her than it was about him.

"Take my cock in your hand—at the base—and stroke me. Harder. You won't break me, don't worry."

Rose didn't break eye contact as she moved her hand up, then down, then up again, in a rhythm that was slow but steady.

"Twist your hand, too," he said, and when she complied,

he groaned. "Yeah, like that. Fuck, Rose, you're driving me crazy."

She stroked him until he wanted to beg her to put him into her mouth, but as if sensing his thoughts, she swirled her tongue around the head of his cock. It was such a light touch that it only made things worse.

God Almighty, he was going to come from just a quick hand job and nothing else. He'd never done that before, but he'd never been this aroused before, either.

Rose took him into her mouth, taking more of him, as she twisted her hand around his cock as she stroked him. The combination of her tongue and her hand and the look in her eyes—the gleam in them that told him she knew she was driving him crazy—plus the feeling of her silky hair in his hand made it all too much.

With a groan, he lifted her face away right as he started to come. His seed shot out in endless bursts, and he swore the entire time. His knees almost buckled.

"Goddamn, Rose," he said as he pulled her up. "Goddamn." He kissed her, thrusting his tongue into her mouth like he wanted to thrust his cock inside her.

She moaned and rubbed against him like a cat in heat. He deepened the kiss until everything else faded but the feel of her soft weight pressing against him.

When he tugged on her hair—a light tug that he barely realized he'd done—she froze. He didn't realize it for a long moment because she kept kissing him, yet the kiss began to fade away as she began to come back to herself.

"No, stop," she whispered. "Stop."

Her voice came to him slowly. It was like hearing someone call out in a tunnel when your eardrums had just been blown out by an explosion. It was rather like when he'd tried to listen for Max's voice after the IED explosion.

"Stop." She pushed him.

He let her go, and she stumbled away from him, breathing hard.

"Rose? What is it?"

He was reminded of a wild animal caught in snare right then: with her eyes wide, her breathing fast, her body trembling. He approached her with cautious steps, his hands up.

"Rose," he said more firmly, "what is it? Are you okay?"

"No, no. I need to go. I need to—what have I done?" She choked back a sob; she slapped a hand to her mouth. "Oh my God, oh my God—"

He tried to get her to stay still, but the second he put his hands on her, she turned wild. She pushed and writhed, her voice shaking, and he'd never been so confused and afraid and hurt as he was right then.

"Talk to me. Baby, *talk to me*. You're safe. It's me—it's Seth."

"Nooooo," she moaned. She clutched her head and collapsed to the floor. She wrapped her arms around her knees.

He didn't touch her again. He waited, letting her panic slow down. After what seemed like an eternity, she seemed to return to herself, although she wouldn't look at him.

"I need to go." She walked like a zombie to the front door without even looking at him. It was like he didn't even exist anymore.

His gut twisted. He reached out to touch her, but she wrenched her arm away. At his hurt look, tears filled her eyes.

"I'm sorry. I'm sorry—just, I need to go. Please. Don't come after me."

She darted away from him and out the door, and when he heard her front door open and then close, he rubbed a hand over his face.

*What the hell have I gotten myself into?*

ose saw Seth and his brothers sit down at a table in the back at The Fainting Goat, and she almost ran into Rebecca when she whirled around.

"Whoa, watch out! I almost dropped my tray." Rebecca glared as she pushed past her.

Rose took a deep breath and forced her heart to slow. She owed Seth an explanation—and an apology. Again. This seemed to be her lot in life: want Seth, offend Seth, avoid Seth. Rinse, repeat ad infinitum.

"DiMarco, you okay?" Ash Younger asked as he walked past her to Trent's office. "You look like you saw a ghost."

She gave him a wan smile. "I'm fine. Sorry, I'll get back to work."

She didn't give a chance for Ash to ask more questions before she hurried into the kitchen, only to realize that there weren't any orders to pick up. She loitered until the chef told her either to start cooking or go be productive.

She checked on her tables, refilled water glasses, and made absolutely certain to avoid any glares directed her way via

Seth Thornton. Considering she refused to look at him, she didn't know if he was glaring. Maybe he was smiling. Maybe he wasn't even looking her way at all.

Oh God, what if he'd decided she wasn't worth the trouble? She couldn't blame him: she kept giving him so many mixed signals *she* was confused.

As she rose from pouring a glass of water, her gaze collided with Seth's. It was inevitable, like they were two magnets attracted to each other no matter how far away the other was.

And Seth wasn't smiling.

He wasn't glaring, either: he seemed speculative. Wary. He raised his glass to her, like an ironic salute.

She gritted her teeth and hurried into the back.

Her dreams had worsened since she'd been with Seth. Not because of what they'd done—which had been beautiful and wonderful and beyond her wildest imaginings—but because the universe seemed bent on not allowing her any respite from Johnny or what he'd done to her. She dreamed of times when she'd considered suicide to escape; she dreamed of when Johnny had toyed with her, acted like he cared about her.

She dreamed of the times when Johnny would pull her hair, and she'd wake up, crying until she fell into an exhausted sleep.

She dreamed that Johnny would have her in the end, no matter what she did.

A cold sweat broke out on her forehead. Shivering, despite the warmth of the restaurant, she went to the ladies' room to put herself back together.

Gazing into the mirror, Rose saw a woman who looked wan and thin, with purple crescents under her eyes. When was the last time she'd felt content? Or safe? She didn't know. Except when she was with Seth, she realized with a pang in her heart, she was barely holding it together.

She brushed strands of hair from her forehead, and after redoing her lipstick, she exited the ladies' room. Only to run into Seth, who stood in front of her like some muscular Great Wall of China.

"It's you," she said, rather inanely. She felt her cheeks grow hot.

"It's me. I didn't think I'd catch you tonight, you know, what with you refusing to even look at me."

She ducked under his arm. "I need to go back to work."

"You have a minute to talk."

She did, but he didn't need to know that. When she saw the pain in his eyes, though, she paused, her heart twisting. She hated that she'd hurt him. If she could take it back, if she could right the wrong she'd done—

"Why do you keep running, Rose?" His voice was quiet, yet indomitable. He crossed his arms over his wide chest and waited.

The words threatened to spill over like a flood after a rainstorm. Memories collided inside her mind, and suddenly, she felt very, very tired. What if she could lay her burdens on someone else for once? Someone strong like Seth?

*He has his own burdens. Don't be selfish, Rose.*

"Look, I'll explain everything to you, but not tonight." At his implacable look, she put her palms up, entreating him. "I promise."

"Why do I feel like your promises are worth less than nothing lately?"

She winced. It hurt, but she deserved that. "You're right. But I can't talk about this here."

Sighing, he pushed his fingers through his hair. "Fine. Tomorrow night? Or are you working?"

"I get off by eight o'clock."

"Good. I'll be home."

They stared at each other, and Rose felt the gulf between them widening. Swallowing, tears imminent, she walked away from him for what felt like the thousandth time.

Throughout the rest of the evening, he didn't try to get her attention. She noticed that he kept his back to her for the most part, although she heard him laugh and joke with his brothers. His brothers, for their part, shot him concerned glances every so often. Rose caught Caleb shaking his head at Harrison, and Harrison frowning into his beer.

When Harrison saw her looking, she whirled away and flew back into the kitchen. She didn't even care if she got reprimanded again for loitering. Better that than having the wrath of three Thornton brothers coming down on her head.

But as fate would have it, Rose couldn't avoid everyone related to Seth that night. Trent popped into the kitchen to steal some fries before the chef shooed him away. Trent grinned like a kid in a candy store.

"Hey, did you see Ash?" he asked Rose offhandedly. "I need to talk to him."

"I saw him earlier. He's probably in your office."

"Great. Thanks, Rose."

She followed him out, but then she found herself on the edges of a family reunion of sorts. Lizzie had Bea, and when Trent saw them, he kissed first his wife, then his daughter on their cheeks.

"I thought you two were heading home?" Trent asked. "I'll be done soon if you want to wait for me."

"Sure. We just stopped by to say hi to everyone." She finally saw Rose standing there. "Oh, hey, Rose! How are you? Too bad you couldn't come out for Caleb's birthday. Heath said you were working."

Trent frowned. He opened his mouth, but then shut it just in time. Rose blushed to the roots of her hair: she'd completely lied about not being able to join the party. She just hadn't had the guts to face all the Thorntons and their significant others in one go.

She gave Lizzie a small wave. "Hi, nice to see you. I should get back to work—"

Seth walked up toward the group, at first not noticing Rose at all. She almost slipped away, but right then, he turned his head. And their gazes met.

Seth nodded at her; Rose froze, torn between running and trying to act like nothing was wrong.

But as luck would have it, Bea would save the day. The baby started to fuss, and when she began to reach out for Seth, Lizzie laughed while Trent shook his head.

"Does somebody want her uncle Seth? Here you go, sweetheart. She missed you."

Seth took his niece without hesitation, and Bea quieted almost instantly. She laid her head on his shoulder, her fist in her mouth as she looked on with those wide baby blue eyes.

Rose's heart melted. It completely melted into a puddle of goo, seeing a big soldier like Seth holding his tiny niece like that. He held her so gently, smiling down at her as he listened to Lizzie and Trent talk, and Rose wished she could give him a reason to smile like that.

If she let herself, she could imagine—oh, all kinds of things. Being with Seth. Loving him. God, even marrying him. And what if, one day, she could place their baby in his arms?

She wanted to cry. When she opened her eyes, she saw Seth watching her, and it was like he *knew*.

"I should get back to work. It was nice seeing all of you," Rose said. As she returned to the kitchen, she could feel Seth's gaze on her shoulders the entire time.

WHEN SETH RETURNED to the table that held his brothers, he felt their collective gazes on him. He drank his beer in silence. They'd acted like they'd wanted to say something all evening, but he wasn't about to help them along.

Lizzie and Trent had left to put Bea to bed, Lizzie whispering that Seth needed to "get his head out of his ass" before patting him on the back. *Helpful,* he thought. As if he were the one giving off a million mixed signals.

As the youngest boy in the family, Seth had been known for pranks—along with Lizzie, his partner in crime—and getting whatever he wanted. Until Jubilee had come along.

Now, Seth felt stupidly young, with his older brothers at turns frowning and then shaking their heads at him. It reminded him of the time he and Lizzie had put a box of toads in their seventh-grade teacher's desk, and they'd been sent home with suspensions in hand. His parents had not been remotely thrilled when they'd gotten that phone call.

Finally, Caleb broke the silence. He was the chattiest of

the three, and Seth cursed Caleb for that particular skill right at that moment.

"So, Seth," Caleb drawled as he flicked a bit of a straw wrapper across the table. "What's up with you?"

Both Mark and Harrison rolled their eyes. Mark took a long drink of his beer while Harrison said, "What he means is: what's going on with you and Rose?"

"Hey, I was trying to be subtle," said Caleb.

Mark said, "You're never subtle."

"Whatever. Seth, just answer the question. We're dying to know."

"More like," said Harrison, "we're *concerned*. You haven't been yourself lately."

Seth almost asked what they knew about him being himself, considering he'd been on three tours back-to-back for the majority of his twenties, but he drank his beer instead. He appreciated that his brothers cared. He just didn't particularly want them to care about this subject.

"Nothing's going on," Seth said, because it was sort of true. One step forward, two steps back: that was their relationship.

"Bullshit." Caleb pointed a finger at him. "We could see everything from over here. You two looked like you were about to climb all over each other right here in the bar."

Seth gaped at Caleb. "Seriously?" was his hoarse reply.

Mark slapped him on the shoulder. "Seriously."

"Shit." Seth put his face in his hands and swore again.

"I know that brotherly advice isn't really what you want right now," said Harrison, "but hear us out. We've been there. Done that. If you have feelings for Rose, don't give up. You'll regret it if you do."

"What do I do if she confuses the hell out of me?" Seth shook his head. "It's not that simple."

"It never is," said Mark. "Women are complicated and we're just their loyal servants. If you manage to find one who loves you—flaws and all—don't let her go."

"Hear, hear," said Caleb as he raised his glass.

They all toasted to that, even Seth. Although at the mention of *love*, his stomach lurched. Was this love? Or the beginnings of it? God, he didn't know. He knew he needed to protect Rose; he knew he wanted to hold her, kiss her, make her his. He wanted to know all her secrets, and God willing, she would know his.

He winced inwardly at that. He'd told her about Max, but sometimes he wasn't sure he was capable of love anymore. It was like war had deadened that part of his soul completely.

He could make love to a woman; he could protect her. But love? Love was something else entirely.

The conversation turned, thankfully, and Seth listened to Caleb talk about Megan and how she kept wanting to redecorate their new house; how Mark's prized mare had just given birth to another foal last week; how Harrison and Sara couldn't agree on any baby names yet.

"She likes old names, like Edith," Harrison said with a laugh. "I asked her if we were having a baby or a grandma, and she refused to speak to me the rest of the afternoon."

"She's the one having the thing. Let her choose the name," said Caleb.

"It's his kid, too." This from Mark. "You'll land on something. If all else fails, name it Sara Jr."

They laughed, even Seth, although his mind was far away. It was still strange to see his siblings get married and have kids.

When had they turned into such mature, responsible adults? Seth almost missed the days when their biggest worry had been whether or not they'd gotten a new Xbox for Christmas.

"You know who you should name the baby after?" said Seth suddenly.

Harrison raised an eyebrow.

"Mom. She'd love you forever if you did."

That made them all groan, Harrison shaking his head with a laugh. They all loved their mother, Lisa, but they also knew very well that she loved to be *involved* in her children's lives.

"I'm surprised she hasn't suggested it herself," said Caleb.

"She has," Harrison deadpanned.

Seth drank his beer. He'd heard all about how Lisa had tried to break up Harrison and Sara when they'd been dating. He hadn't been surprised, but he had been surprised to see Lisa become somewhat subdued when Seth had returned from abroad.

When the brothers said goodbye, Seth looked for Rose, but according to one of the waitresses, she'd already headed home.

Of course she had. Hummingbirds were difficult creatures to catch.

CHAPTER THIRTEEN

R ose had never hated not having a car more than when Heath called her to tell her his place had been broken into. He'd told her she didn't need to come over, but of course she would. He was her brother, for God's sake.

The bus system in Fair Haven was mediocre at best. Deciding to pay for an Uber even though she really couldn't spare the cash, Rose arrived about fifteen minutes later at Heath's small bungalow on the south side of town. One of the few benefits of living in a small town was that you didn't get stuck in traffic just driving a handful of miles away.

There was a Fair Haven police car outside Heath's house, and she approached to see Caleb Thornton talking with Heath.

"Rose! I told you didn't need to come," Heath admonished, but he didn't look upset.

She hugged him hard, and he laughed.

"I'm fine. I wasn't even here, and they didn't take anything that I can find. Just messed up the place."

That only made her feel worse. When she started shaking, Heath made her look him in the eye.

She knew this had to have been Johnny. She had no idea what he'd been looking for, but he knew he could hurt her through Heath. He'd always known it. Her heart pounded, adrenaline making her jittery.

"We'll keep an eye out for any suspicious activity," Caleb said, "but it's strange that nothing was taken."

Heath nodded. "Thanks. I'll let you know."

Caleb glanced at Rose and frowned. "Are you okay, ma'am? You look pale."

She tried a tremulous smile, but she probably looked so ghastly that it was rather terrifying. Heath took her arm and led her inside. "Call me if you need anything else," he called to Caleb over his shoulder.

Heath had Rose sit down on the couch before pressing a glass of water into her hand.

"Were you done talking to Caleb? You shouldn't have sent him away," she said.

"He got what he needed. Now, why did you come here when I told you not to?"

She drank the water to figure out how to answer that question. She needed to tell Heath what was going on with Johnny. That morning, she'd tallied up her latest paycheck from The Fainting Goat and had almost sobbed with relief: she had enough to pay back Johnny. This would all be over soon.

She finished her water, mostly to still her trembling. Taking Heath's hand, she squeezed it.

"I've been meaning to talk to you for a while now. I just haven't had the courage to say the words," she began.

"What is this all about?"

How to explain? How to tell him without upsetting him? She took a deep breath.

"Johnny has been…contacting me. Lately."

It was like a bomb went off in the living room. Heath pulled his hand away and stared at her.

"How long?" he rasped.

"Since mid-June. He found me here."

"Tell me you went to the police. Tell me you didn't talk to that creep. Tell me, please."

Rose smiled sadly. "That same creep who saved you from going to jail and ruining your life?"

That made Heath stand up, and as he began to pace, Rose could sense the barely leashed tension inside him.

"Tell me the truth for once. I knew you hid from me what really happened with that bastard." His voice was modulated, but rage teased at the edges. The calm and collected teacher had disappeared.

"Only if you don't stand in front of me, glaring at me. Sit down. It's hard enough telling you this without you looking like you'd enjoy strangling me."

"Don't give me ideas."

When the words came, they came haltingly. She tried to downplay what Johnny had done at first, as she'd always done. Heath didn't say a word. He stared at a spot on the couch and listened.

"When you were arrested, he told me he could help you. So I said yes to whatever he wanted."

Heath dropped his face into his hands, and Rose wondered if he hated her now. He didn't make a sound for a long moment, until finally, he groaned like a wounded animal.

When he looked up, she saw, to her shock, that he had tears in his eyes.

"Don't try to spare me. Tell me what he did. *Tell me.*"

She swallowed. Then: "He raped me. Is that what you wanted to hear? I didn't realize that was what it was at the time, but I do now."

Heath swore. He seemed to collapse in on himself right then and there, and Rose realized for the first time what her sacrifice would do to *him*. She had never wanted him to shoulder a burden that had been her choice.

Choice? She almost laughed. Johnny hadn't allowed that. He'd used her fears and her love for her brother for his own twisted mind games.

"God, *God.*" Heath stood up again and paced. "I knew something had happened, but I didn't want to believe it. And to get me out of going to prison?" He whirled on Rose, his face so stark, so grief-stricken, that it made Rose's heart bleed. "I would've rather gone to prison than to have had that happen to you."

"How could I? You had your entire future ahead of you. You were so close to becoming a teacher, and then you were arrested for a crime you didn't even commit! You took care of me for our whole lives; you gave up so much for me. How could I not have done the same?"

Heath just shook his head. Finally, after a long moment of silence, he asked, "What does Johnny want now? And why haven't you gone to the police?"

She explained that she'd saved enough money to pay Johnny back, and that she hadn't gone to the police because she knew very well there was nothing they could do. And it would hurt Heath if it got out that he'd been arrested on drug charges.

"Rose, are you *insane*? He could hurt you again, or worse, kill you!" He pulled his phone from his back pocket. "I'm calling Caleb to tell him what's really going on—"

"No, you can't!" She grabbed his phone. "Please, don't. I'll make this all end. You'll see. And then he'll be out of our lives forever."

"Oh, Rose," Heath said with a head shake. "You can't still be this naïve. You know what guys like that will do. His word isn't worth anything."

She knew that. *She knew that.* But what did he want her to do? If she went to the police, she'd have to tell them all about Johnny's abuse. And then what? It would be a case of he said, she said. Johnny had enough friends in high places that any charges like that against him would be quickly swept under the rug.

Rose wasn't naïve—not anymore. She knew this was her last opportunity to put an end to all of this.

Maybe that was why she carried a gun; she'd always known this would end with either getting Johnny to see sense or defending herself against the man who would never stop hunting her.

"Just trust me," she said, gazing into her brother's eyes. "That's all I'm asking. I told you about all this because I wanted you to know." Her eyes filled with tears. "I love you, Heath. You're my brother. I'd do anything for you."

He sighed and pulled her into a tight hug. She buried her face in his shoulder, soaking his shirt with her tears.

"I love you. God, this was why you disappeared for those years? When you wouldn't talk to me? I should've known.

Hell, I think I did know. I just didn't want to believe it." He gripped her tighter. "If anyone was a coward, it was me."

"You? No. I wouldn't let you find me. I knew you were looking for me. You never gave up, did you?"

His smile was twisted. "No, I didn't. And when you finally called me and said you'd move here…" He rested his chin on the top of her head. "I was happier than I'd ever been in my life."

"I'm sorry I ran away from you. I was ashamed."

He sighed. "Then from now on, I'll carry that shame for you. It should be my burden to bear, not yours."

"No, it's not your burden, and it's not mine." She wiped her eyes, sniffling. "The person who should be judged is Johnny. He's the reason for all of this. He's hurt so many people. Don't take the shame that should be his and make it yours."

That made Heath smile sadly. "When did you become so wise?"

"I had to grow up to survive."

He flinched, and she wished she hadn't said that. But it was true: although she'd been almost twenty-one, she'd still been so young and sheltered when she'd met Johnny. She'd been ripe for the plucking, and Johnny had *known*.

Men like him always knew.

"I hate that you felt like you couldn't tell me," Heath said as they sat back down on the couch. "I want you to know you can always come to me about anything."

She felt so drained that she could sleep for the rest of her life, but her confession had helped the shadows recede somewhat. They would never go away—she knew that. Yet having someone to talk to helped her more than she could've realized.

She leaned her head against Heath's shoulder. "Anything? Even if I want to join a traveling circus?"

"Do those still exist?"

"I think so. I'm not sure what I'd be, though. Trapeze artist? Lion tamer?"

"How about you stay here in Fair Haven and try out some other job that's a little less dangerous?"

She nodded, yawning. They sat companionably for a little while longer. She'd missed this with Heath, and during the years when she'd avoided him, she'd thought about him constantly. If he was happy; if he hated her for running from him. She'd expected him to hate her still when she'd moved to Fair Haven, but she was glad to have been wrong.

"I didn't tell you this, but when I was at Caleb's birthday party last weekend, Caleb let something slip about his brother."

Rose stilled. "Which one?"

"I'm sure you can guess. He said that sometimes they all feel like Seth is a stranger, since he's been gone for so many years. But he thinks that the reason Seth hasn't wandered off again is not because of the family, but because of someone else."

"Oh?"

"What I'm trying to say and doing horribly at is: that if you care about Seth…" Heath swallowed, clearly uncomfortable now. "You shouldn't let him go. Don't let Johnny win, Rosie. He isn't worth it."

She didn't know what to say to that. She was surprised that Heath would say anything positive about Seth. Hadn't he warned her away from him more than once?

As if he'd read her mind, his mouth twisted into a smile. "I know. I told you to watch out for those Thorntons. Maybe my own bias was getting in the way because you're my sister. Can you blame me?"

"Maybe." She sighed. "I don't know if I am brave enough," she admitted.

Heath jostled her shoulder. "Of course you are. You're the bravest person I know. If there's a way, you'll find it. I believe it."

She smiled. She hoped she could find the same confidence in herself as Heath had.

CHAPTER FOURTEEN

That night, Rose lay in her nest of blankets with Callie and thought. She thought about everything she'd told Heath, and everything he'd told her.

*You can't let fear rule your life.*

Those words thrummed in her mind like a single chord of music. She stroked Callie as she thought, and considered, and finally, made a decision.

She knew very well it wouldn't be as easy as letting go and dusting her hands of everything that had happened. But that didn't mean she should stay in a kind of stasis, either.

If she didn't push herself to move forward, no one would.

It was close to midnight. She wondered if Seth was asleep, but then she heard the creak of footsteps next door.

The universe was giving her a sign, that was for sure.

"I'll be back later," she whispered to Callie. Before she left, she brushed her teeth—a second time—brushed her hair, put on her prettiest bra-and-panty set, and then added a little lipstick on top of it all.

If she was going to seduce a man, she might as well give it her best shot.

When she stood outside Seth's door, she almost lost her nerve. But before she could hightail it and run, he swung the door open and then crossed his arms over his chest.

Rose cleared her throat. "Can I come in?"

"How many times are we going to do this?" was his reply.

She winced. It wasn't cold out, but she shivered nonetheless. She suddenly felt silly, with her fluffed hair and lipstick, standing outside Seth's door like he would've fallen at her feet in an instant.

"I told you I'd tell you what was going on," she said. "So, here I am."

"It's midnight."

"I thought I'd continue our usual trend of nighttime sessions."

He raised an eyebrow, and then he moved aside so she could come in. She ducked under his arm before he could change his mind and lock her out.

Tonight he wore a shirt, which was a shame. Then again, it would help her concentrate. Closing her eyes, she centered herself and took a deep breath. She started to shiver, though, and she wondered if she was going to be sick.

It didn't help that she'd already told all of this to Heath earlier. The thought of explaining *again*? She wasn't sure she had the strength to do that.

When she opened her eyes, she saw Seth's concern. He led her to the couch, his touch gentle.

"You don't have to tell me anything." He held up a hand at her protest. "That was unfair of me. That's not to say I would stop you if you wanted to tell me, of course. But you look like you're about to puke."

She laughed and tugged at her hair. "You could say that."

"Then just sit with me." In a tone that was almost shy, he added, "I missed you."

That sent her hormones into overdrive. Gazing at him now, with his dark hair rumpled and smelling of soap from a recent shower, she wanted to crawl onto his lap and kiss him until everything else faded away.

He still held her hand. Gathering her courage, she took his hand and pressed it to her breast. He stilled.

"If we aren't going to talk, I'd rather we enjoy ourselves." She licked her lips. "I've missed you, too. In fact, all I've wanted lately is you."

His eyes flashed in the dim light from a nearby lamp. "Hummingbird…"

"No, don't. I know what I want. I know I've been confusing the hell out of you, and all I can say is that things are complicated, but you know what isn't complicated?" She asked this as she climbed into his lap, his hand still on her breast.

"What isn't complicated?" he asked hoarsely.

"How much I want you."

His eyes flashed, and then in a quick movement, she pulled her tank top off and tossed it over her shoulder, baring the bright blue bra she'd bought on a whim years ago. His hand that had held her breast now gripped her waist.

Bending toward him, she cupped his stern face in her hands. "Make love to me," she whispered against his lips.

It was like those words unleashed him. With a growl, he tangled his fingers into her hair and kissed her, his tongue pushing into her mouth within seconds. She gasped, loving the taste of him, the feeling of his tongue against her own.

That hand on her waist moved upward to cup her breast.

"Say it again," he commanded. "Tell me how much you want me."

"More than anything."

He smiled a smile that she imagined would be called predatory—like the wildcat she'd compared him to when she'd first met him.

He kissed her harder before kissing down her throat. When he reached her sternum, he made quick work of pushing off her bra straps to reveal her breasts. Her nipples strained toward him, and when he enclosed one nipple in his mouth, she bit her lip to keep from crying out.

With his tongue and his teeth and his lips, he paid homage to one breast and then the other, just like he had all those nights ago. Except in this instance, Rose knew this was only the beginning of their night together.

"I love your breasts. God, you're beautiful."

Rose laughed breathily. "Do you just love my breasts?"

She'd meant it jokingly, but his expression turned serious for a quick second. But whatever had descended into his mind was quickly pushed aside, and Rose found herself toppled onto the couch and underneath Seth.

He stripped out of his shirt as she took off her bra, needing to feel him skin to skin. The hardness of his chest against her sensitive breasts made her moan and writhe. It didn't help that his fingers were skimming the soft skin of her pelvis below her shorts and panties.

His cock—like an iron bar—pressed against her belly as

he danced his fingers across her sex. She closed her eyes and gave into the pleasure of his touch.

It was strange: she'd thought having a man as big and strong as Seth on top of her, dominating her, would've made her panic, yet she only felt safe in his arms. A lump formed in her throat, and as he touched her with such tenderness, she felt perilously close to tears.

Seth played with her, fondling her sex, his strokes light as a moth's wings, and she felt her core tighten. He avoided her swollen clit, though, and when he pressed a finger inside of her, she cried out.

"Touch me—no, higher. Higher. *Seth*."

"I know, baby, but I don't want you to come without me." He stroked her sex one last time before pulling her shorts and panties all the way off.

He moved up her body and kissed her before saying, "I'll be right back."

She blinked, dazed from the onslaught of pleasure. When Seth returned, he flashed a foil pack in his hand. "Probably don't want to forget this," he said. "Put it on me?"

It took her a moment to tear the packet open—her body was shaking, and her brain was mush—but after a few tries and some assistance from Seth, they got the condom on. Rose stroked his cock the way she'd learned he liked, shooting him an impish grin.

"Do you want this to be over before it's even begun?" He kissed her hard, probably just to distract her so he could get her under him.

Rose had no complaints there.

Yet with his weight over her, the smell and taste of him enveloping her senses, she started shaking for an entirely different reason. She fought against the panic, but it was like clawing through a fog: she couldn't hang onto it to push it away. She gasped for breath when he touched her knee; she felt dizzy, disoriented.

"Wait, wait," she burst out. "Just give me a minute."

Seth stilled. He didn't ask questions, for which she was infinitely grateful, but instead sat next to her, not touching. She sat up, but she had to put her head between her knees. God, this was embarrassing! Was she going to *faint* before having sex with the man she loved?

She groaned for another reason: she loved him. *She loved him.* She wanted him, too, and her body still thrummed with desire, yet her mind fought that desire, tooth and nail. Why couldn't she get her body and her mind to align for once?

"Rose, you're scaring me. Talk to me." She heard Seth's voice from a distance. Then: "We don't have to do anything else tonight."

"No!" She almost yelled the word. It seemed to echo in the small space. Wincing, she said more quietly, "No, I want this. I want you." She was panting, and then she was climbing into his lap before she could let the panic take over again.

"I want you more than I've ever wanted anyone in my whole life," she whispered against his lips. She stroked her hands down his chest, and he shuddered. His cock bobbed between them, a reminder of how much he wanted *her*.

Rose knew she couldn't let what Johnny had done to her stop her from living. *Don't live your life in fear.*

"Can I be in charge?" Rose asked. She tried to smile, but it felt forced.

Seth was nonplussed, but when he nodded and didn't touch her, she found herself falling in love with him even more. She didn't deserve this man, but she vowed she would try to be worthy of him.

Setting her hands on his shoulders, she maneuvered between them until she took hold of his cock. He hissed, and she almost dropped him when he said, "No, don't stop. Don't ever stop."

Slowly, and somewhat awkwardly, she lodged the tip of him in her entrance, and inch by inch, she took him inside. It was a tight fit, and Rose was certain she couldn't take any more of him when she slid down a little further. Finally, he was lodged to the hilt, and Rose couldn't stop gasping.

It was too much, yet never enough. She laid her head on his shoulder for a moment. She couldn't stop shaking, but this time, it wasn't out of fear. The fear seemed to have crept away —for now.

She'd take the respite, no matter how short-lived it was.

Rose began to rise up and down, riding him in a leisurely rhythm, and all the while, Seth didn't touch her. Tipping her head back, she concentrated solely on the feeling of his cock inside her, the sound of his breathing, the smell of his sweat. Her nails dug into his shoulders, and he bucked a little.

The orgasm that had begun to twist and turn inside of her earlier returned, and before she knew it, she was bouncing on him faster and faster. Chasing her release with every stroke.

Seth said her name, swearing, and Rose took his hands and placed them on her breasts. He kissed her, the kiss wild in its intensity, as they both chased their own peaks. He thumbed her nipples, which sent sensations of pleasure straight to her core.

She was so close—so close. When Seth bit the side of her neck, the sharp nip was all that she needed to come right then.

She shouted his name, panting and gasping, and it was only his arms around her that kept her upright.

"Fuck, Rose, so good," he said, and then a few moments later she felt his cock twitch and he was coming, too, his own orgasm seemingly endless.

She felt float-y, light, and she laughed. She laughed until Seth gave her a strange look, but then he was smiling, too. She hugged him close and kissed him. This resulted in him telling her that if she kept that up, he'd have her all over again in the next few minutes.

"I wouldn't mind," she admitted. Seth just groaned.

He carried her to his bedroom after that, going to the bathroom to get rid of the condom and return with a washcloth for them both. She could barely move, her mind and her body languid. Could bones melt? Because she was fairly certain hers had.

Seth got into bed with her and slung an arm around her waist. The feel of his breath on her neck, the way his fingers traced light patterns on her belly, and the sound of his breathing when he fell asleep all came together to feel almost unbearably intimate.

She'd never slept with a man before—not literally. Not like this.

The tears came without warning. They spilled onto the pillow, and Rose bit her tongue to keep from making any noise. She wasn't sure if these were tears of release or tears of regret or both. Maybe they were just tears to wash away everything ugly that had happened to her.

*I'll never regret loving Seth,* she thought. This night had been the most beautiful of her life, yet that didn't stop that old friend of hers—panic—from coming back around again. It always did.

She forced herself not to bolt, though, and she prayed that this wave would pass until she could sleep as peacefully as Seth was right now. Memories of Johnny mixed together with the memories of tonight, and that made her stomach churn. She couldn't bear having Johnny taint this.

Rose closed her eyes and took one deep breath, and then another. She wiped away the tears, although a few stray ones still spilled over. When she was certain Seth was fast asleep, she rose from the bed and went to the bathroom to rinse her face in cold water. She brushed her teeth for good measure upon finding an extra toothbrush, because it made this seem normal. It made *her* seem normal.

She'd been a virgin when Johnny had raped her. In her mind, she'd still been a virgin until tonight. That made her smile. What woman would regret giving her virginity to a man as handsome and amazing as Seth Thornton? Certainly not her. She was glad that this time, it was her choice—and only her choice.

When she returned to Seth's bed, she smiled: she could just make out his sleeping face. He seemed so much younger when he was asleep. She prayed that he wouldn't awaken with any nightmares, and she prayed that she wouldn't either.

Climbing in beside him, she placed his arm back over her like a protective shield and then laced their fingers together. He mumbled something in his sleep before she felt sleep claim her, too.

CHAPTER FIFTEEN

Rose knew her happiness couldn't last. The morning after, she went to her apartment to shower and get ready for work. Seth had made it difficult for her to leave, though, as he'd kept kissing her and luring her back into bed. After they'd eaten breakfast, he'd carried her to his bed again, the sex slow and tender and so amazing Rose couldn't believe any of it was real.

Toweling her hair dry, she heard her phone ring. Her heart beat in excitement, thinking it was Seth, but when she saw it was an unknown number, her heart sank.

"Hello?" she answered. She refused to sound scared.

"Rosie, it's been too long. I got your message," said Johnny, his voice almost jovial. "I'd love to meet with you, but I don't have much time to waste. How about Saturday afternoon, at the Sanditon Pass?"

"That's at least an hour away. I don't have a car—"

"Figure it out." His jovial tone melted away. "Either agree to meet me there, or you can kiss your boyfriend and your brother goodbye."

"And what if I say no?" She didn't know why she was trying to provoke him. Maybe because she was just so tired of capitulating to his demands.

He laughed. "You already know what'll happen. Do you want everyone to know what your brother did? Or for him to lose his precious job because of you?"

She remained silent, seething.

"That's what I thought. I'll text you the exact address. Oh, and Rosie?"

"What?"

"Come alone. Don't tell anyone where you're going. Believe me, if I catch a whiff of you blabbing, you'll regret it."

"Fine," she replied. "But I have one more question."

"Of course you do."

"Did you break into Heath's place?"

Johnny didn't reply for a long moment, and Rose could imagine him shrugging. "Does it matter?" he countered.

"No, I guess it doesn't."

She sat in her apartment with Callie's head in her lap. Taking out her box from her safe, she counted the money in it for what felt like the thousandth time. It was enough—more than enough. Johnny didn't deserve a penny of it, but it was her last chance to get him to stop this. Money was always a safe bet to get people to leave you alone.

She considered going next door to tell Seth about Johnny's demands, but she hesitated. She knew Johnny; she knew he watched her and the people around her. And would Seth agree to stay quiet? Or not to follow her to Sanditon Pass?

Unlikely, if not impossible.

By the time she arrived at work a few hours later, she was so distracted that Rebecca asked her what was going on.

"You've forgotten refills and brought out the wrong orders," Rebecca said, assessing Rose. "You look like hell."

Rose laughed, but it was a hollow sound. "Just a lot on my mind. If anyone complains, tell them it was all my fault."

When one customer became upset that his steak was cooked well-done instead of medium rare, Rose almost bit her tongue in half trying to keep her cool. Normally the annoying customers didn't ruffle her, but she was on a short fuse at the moment. She almost wished Johnny would show up so she could punch him. Instead, she kept the anger balled up inside for the time being.

Exhausted and wanting nothing more than to sleep for days, Rose left work with her mind elsewhere. Yet when someone stepped out of the shadows, saying her name, she pulled her gun out without a second thought.

The dim light revealed the shadowy figure was Seth. He blinked at the gun.

"I thought we'd moved past this?" he joked.

When she didn't say anything, just put the gun back into her jacket pocket, he touched her arm.

"Hey, what was that about? I told you that I'd walk you home from work, especially at night."

She shrugged, embarrassed. "Reflex, I guess," she replied.

He narrowed his eyes at her, but she looked away.

"Can we go home? I'm exhausted," she said.

They didn't speak as they walked back to their apartment complex. Everything seemed so pointless right then, and it made her shoulders slump. How could she love Seth when she couldn't be honest with him? When she was afraid he would hate her if he discovered what she'd done?

A lump formed in her throat as they arrived at their apartments. Before she could lose her nerve, she asked him, "Want to come in?"

He nodded and followed her in.

Callie rose and greeted them both. Callie had decided that she approved of Seth, and to Rose's amusement, the dog seemed to love Seth more than Rose at this point. Callie panted, her tongue hanging out, and her tail wagging so fast it was a total blur.

Rose couldn't tell Seth about her promise to Johnny, but she could tell him everything else. The things she'd told Heath recently.

She almost laughed. Apparently her fate lately was to tell the men in her life how one man in particular had almost destroyed her life completely.

After sleeping together last night, Seth had gotten her to agree to let him buy her a futon for her living room that following morning., This was the first night she would use it for a bed. She sat down on it now, the wood creaking when Seth sat beside her.

"I told you that I'd explain everything to you," she said. "About Johnny."

He stilled. "Hummingbird, you don't have to tell me anything you don't want to."

"That's the thing: I want you to know." *Because if you can't love me anymore, I want to know now.* "And I said I'd explain everything."

His eyes darkened, and he looked like he wanted to take her into his arms. But right then, she needed to stand on her own two feet—metaphorically speaking.

"Before you start," he said with a small smile, "let's have something to drink."

Ten minutes later, Seth drank a beer while Rose sipped at a glass of wine. Since telling Heath what had happened, she found that the words weren't as difficult to come by.

She didn't sugarcoat any of it: she told him exactly what she'd told Heath. About Heath's arrest, her deal with Johnny. How she'd thought Johnny was her savior, but he'd turned out to be her tormenter. She recounted the abuse and the rapes, and she closed her eyes for a moment when she saw Seth's anger at her words.

"He's been stalking me now, but I haven't seen him in a while," she said. It was mostly true: she hadn't *seen* him in a while.

Seth frowned, but he was so distracted by her story that he didn't poke holes in that part of it. Instead, she saw a man who looked both frozen and enraged. His soldier's training seemed to keep him from exploding completely. The only evidence of his agitation was how he clenched and unclenched his fist against his knee.

"That's my story," she said sadly. She shrugged. "I was an idiot to think Johnny would take care of me."

"No, you weren't." The words seemed to burst from Seth. "You wanted to believe that he'd help you. You weren't stupid, he was a bastard. An evil, cruel bastard."

Seth hissed in a breath, and when Rose saw his eyes, she could honestly say she'd never seen a man so angry yet so contained at the same time. She swallowed, her mouth dry.

"Fuck!" He growled the word as he rose from the futon. He paced, much like Heath had paced, but while Heath had been stricken with guilt, Seth was a caged animal.

"Fuck him. Goddamn, Rose, if I ever see him, I'll kill him." It wasn't just a threat, she knew—it was a promise.

"You'll have to get in line after me." She got up and put her arms around him. "I was so afraid to tell you," she admitted, speaking to his chest. "I was afraid you'd hate me for it."

He inhaled. "Hate *you* for it? Jesus, Rose. You've gone through so much, yet you're still so kind and lovely. You're the most amazing woman I've ever met." He tipped up her chin so she could look into his eyes. "If anything, I don't deserve to kiss your feet."

A watery smile touched her lips, and Seth gently brushed away the tears that fell from her eyes. She laid her cheek against his chest, hearing his heart thump. It was a comforting sound, reminding her of how precious life was. How precious Seth's life was to her.

She wanted to tell him she loved him, but she hesitated. She hadn't told him everything; it seemed unfair of her to admit to her feelings when she couldn't be fully honest with him.

"I want to make love to you," he whispered in her ear. He sounded unsure, like he didn't have any right to ask her that.

Stepping away from him, Rose smiled. "Then what are you waiting for?"

SETH HAD NEVER SAID those words before, but it was true. He wanted to make love to her. He wanted to show her how amazing she was, how she should never blame herself for what had happened to her.

For what Johnny had done to her—it hadn't been some random force. A man had hurt her, and when Seth had said he'd kill Johnny, he hadn't lied. The only thing stopping him from going after Johnny right that moment was the look in Rose's eyes as she started to undress in front of him.

She pulled off her shirt to reveal a white bra that had seen better days: frayed and with one strap held up with a safety pin, it was clearly past its expiration date. But Seth didn't care, she was beautiful in rags or the most expensive clothes in existence.

She unhooked her bra before unzipping her jeans that hugged every curve. Her panties were a scrap of cotton, and Seth could make out the dark hair covering her sex through the fabric. He swallowed, his cock pulsing against his jeans.

Rose sent him a shy smile, a flush covering her chest up to her cheeks. Her nipples were a dark pink—rose-colored, which was appropriate—and in the overhead light, he noticed a constellation of freckles on her stomach.

She finally stripped out of her panties and moved toward him. She placed her hands on his chest, but he waited for her to let him know he could touch her in turn. After what she'd told him, he understood why she'd freaked out when they'd first had sex. Anger thrummed in his blood, but then Rose nuzzled him, sighing softly.

"You're my first, you know," she said. She tipped her head back to look at him. "My *real* first. You know what I mean?"

He did, and it staggered him. He wished he had known. He would've gone more slowly. He would've savored her. But he couldn't regret any of it, and when he gazed into her eyes, he knew she didn't regret it, either.

Seth touched her silky dark hair, fingering the blue tips. "I'm honored," he said seriously. "I can guarantee that your third, fourth, fifth—one hundredth—time with me will be fucking fantastic."

She giggled. "One hundred times? How about one thousand?"

"Deal."

He picked her up, avoiding the rickety futon she'd barely let him buy for her, and pushed her against the nearest wall. They both made short work of his clothes, and when her slim fingers encircled his cock, he almost knocked his forehead on the wall in front of him.

She'd gotten way too good at that—she squeezed and stroked as she began to kiss his chest, licking at his nipples. He, in turn, sucked at her neck until he left a small mark. She tasted like woman and a salty-sweetness he couldn't identify.

He loved the way she said his name, her voice throaty, and how she reacted so strongly to every touch and caress. She was a live-wire in his arms, and in turn, she electrified him.

When he kneeled in front of her, he pushed her legs apart until he could see her. Smell her. She was as pink here as her nipples, and he watched in fascination as her entire body turned a similar shade of pink.

Rose's fingers tangled in his hair as he licked her in one slow stroke. Her head hit the wall with a thunk, but she only dug her fingers harder into his scalp, egging him on.

"Why are you so good at that? It's not fair. You drive me crazy." She panted, talking nonsense. If Seth weren't otherwise preoccupied, he would've laughed.

She swore at him, curse words dropping like dirty gemstones from her tongue, and it only made him want to make her insane with want. He nuzzled her, lapping at her, and before long, he was circling her clit with his tongue as he edged a finger around her entrance.

"Oh my God, oh my God. Just like that. No, nooooo." She

squealed when he pushed his finger totally inside her, and then she moaned so loudly that she clapped a hand over her mouth.

He could feel her thighs trembling, and he knew she was close. With one more lap of his tongue and a twist of his finger, she came. Her sheath contracted as her body spasmed, and he heard her gasp his name before she let out a high-pitched scream. Or yelp. It was hard to tell.

Seth kissed her thighs, her hip, the constellation of freckles on her belly. He thanked his own forward thinking that he'd put a condom in his wallet the day before, and he had the condom on before Rose even noticed.

Rose glanced down at his cock. "Oh, you had a condom? That's good, because I don't have any." She giggled.

He kissed the tip of her nose, her mouth. Pulling her legs up and around his hips, he opened her to him. Her heat seared him, and it was all he could do not to plunge inside her.

"I want you inside me." Her voice was a hot whisper in his ear. "I want you so much, Seth."

A second later, he pushed inside her in one stroke until he was lodged to the hilt. Rose dug her nails into his shoulders—she tended to do this every time he was inside her, and he loved it—and then they were kissing as he thrust.

Gripping her thighs, he heard them knocking against the wall with each thrust, but he didn't care if the entire apartment complex heard them. All he cared about was how extraordinary she felt around him, and how he knew right then that he could never let her go.

"I'm close. Fuck, Rose." He angled his thrusts so his pelvis pressed against her clit. When he hit the perfect angle, he watched as her eyes rolled back inside her head.

Bingo.

"Keep going, faster, faster, harder, yes, God, Seth!" she yelled when her second orgasm hit.

Seth grunted, sweat beading on his forehead. His own release was close—so close—and when Rose licked his jaw, he felt his body tense. His orgasm hit him with the subtlety of a bomb going off. He slapped a hand against the wall, his body shaking until his muscles and bones all turned to jelly.

They stood like that for a long moment, breathing hard, when Seth felt something cold between his ass cheeks. He jumped, yelping.

Rose burst out laughing. "Callie! No! Leave Seth alone. Go lie down." She laughed even harder at his expression.

Seth set Rose down as he turned to glare at her dog. "Can't a guy get a little respect around here?"

"Aw, she didn't mean it. Did you?" Rose rubbed Callie's nose and bent to kiss her ears. Callie just gave her a wide doggy smile.

After cleaning up, they pulled out Rose's futon and curled up together. Although the sex was amazing, Seth had to admit he liked this part almost as much. Which meant he was turning into a total sap. He could just imagine what Max would've said: *Watch out. You're not getting out of that trap anytime soon, man.*

Seth moved his hand under his pillow, only to find a book there. He pulled it out. *North and South* by Elizabeth Gaskell.

"Oh, I'd forgotten I'd put that there." Rose took the book from him, smiling. "This is one of my favorites." Her eyes widened. "The hero's name is Mr. Thornton, actually. John Thornton."

Seth lay on his back, his hands behind his head. "What a coincidence. Is he ridiculously good-looking and a total lady-killer?"

"He's actually really awkward. He totally screws up the first marriage proposal to Margaret and she tells him to take a hike." Her smile turned dreamy. "He's so romantic."

Seth snorted. He flipped through the book, intrigued despite himself. "Have you read all of the books on your bookshelf?"

"Mostly. A lot of them I got in college…"

At the mention of college, they both stilled. Because of Johnny, Rose hadn't finished college, had she? Seth hated Johnny even more, which he didn't think was possible.

"You were an English major?"

"Yeah. Sometimes I think about going back."

He rubbed her arm. "Why not? You should."

"I don't know. I'm too old, and it would be weird…"

"It's never too late. Besides, you love it. Who reads books like this? Nobody, except people who really love them."

She lay down on her stomach, her hair falling down her back in dark waves. "And then what? I teach? Write books?"

"Whatever you want. Sing songs in the park if you want. As long as it makes you happy."

They talked into the night: about Seth, growing up in his crazy family; about Rose, growing up without a father and then without either parent. They talked about what they'd wanted to be when they were kids and how their lives had turned out so differently. Seth told her about when Lizzie had run off, and how he'd been adrift until he'd joined the Marines.

He didn't tell her about possibly returning for another tour. He didn't know why—or maybe he did. Maybe he didn't want her to know that he was afraid he could only be a soldier and nothing else. That war was in his blood, and if he wasn't in the Marines, he became adrift, just like he'd been before he'd joined up.

Yet as they lay together, Seth also knew that he couldn't let Rose go. He had convinced himself he couldn't love, that Max's death had killed that part of him, but more and more, he realized he'd been wrong.

He loved her. He closed his eyes against the realization, but there it was. He'd do anything for her, and wasn't that love in its purest form?

When her breathing became even and slow, he kissed her pale shoulder. *I love you*, he thought, unsure if he could ever say the words aloud.

# CHAPTER SIXTEEN

Rose awoke to the sound of Seth's voice. Yawning, she sat up, her brain slowly clearing of sleep.

Seth's shoulders were tense as he spoke to someone on the phone. "Yeah, you'll have my answer soon, sir. Yeah. Yeah, I understand. Bye."

He seemed not to realize she was next to him. She began to rub his shoulders, concerned, but he pushed her hands away.

"I need to take a shower," he muttered. "I'll be back," he added in a gentler voice.

Rose heard the water turn on next door, and as she made breakfast for herself and Seth, she frowned. Who wanted an answer from him? He hadn't mentioned anything of the sort lately.

Rose gave Callie a bite of bacon. "It's just one thing after another with us, isn't it?"

Seth returned twenty minutes later, his hair wet and looking a little less dazed. They sat down to eat, not speaking, and Rose decided not to press him until he felt ready to tell her what was going on.

Seth set his plate down on the table, smiling when Callie tried to nose another piece of bacon from his plate. "Sit," Seth said, and after Callie sat, he gave her a piece as a reward.

"I guess you're wondering what that was about," he said finally.

Rose bit her lip and began to fiddle with her hair. "Something like that."

He sighed, running his hands through his hair, disheveling the damp strands. "My CO told me that he has a mission in mind for me. He can get me switched from inactive duty to active by the fall if I accept."

"I don't understand."

"It means I'd do a fourth tour."

Rose swallowed. She felt dizzy at the news, like her world had been tilted on its axis. Seth could be leaving in only a few months? She closed her eyes and did her best to stave off the panic.

"Do you know what you're going to say?" she asked woodenly.

"No. Sometimes I think I should, because what the hell am I doing here? Making tables?" At her hurt look, he winced. "I don't mean you. I'm sorry. I just meant that I feel like I'm meant to be only a soldier and nothing else."

"That's not true. You did really well in the Marines, from what you've told me, but you can't go to war for the rest of your life. We might not even have any wars to go to eventually." They both stared at each other at that statement before laughing sadly.

"Okay, maybe not," she allowed, "and I may know

nothing about the military, but you don't stay on the front lines forever. Right?"

"Right. After Max died, I thought I was done." Seth leaned back, sighing. "But I don't know anymore. Sergeant Loyd has offered me something that could make me a sergeant if things go well."

"And if things go badly?" Her voice was a whisper now. "What happens if you don't come back?"

"I came back three times already. What's a fourth?"

His light tone fell flat, and they both said nothing. The panic once again clawed at Rose's mind. She'd just found Seth —fallen in love with him—and here he was, about to leave her.

The thought sent her to a dark place, where she was alone no matter what she did.

"Rose," he said as he lifted up her chin. "It's going to be all right. I haven't made my decision yet anyway."

"Haven't you, though? If you were going to say no, you would've already."

He couldn't deny it; he dropped his hand and clenched his jaw.

"I don't have a right to tell you what to do with your life, but think about your family. Yourself, even. You still have nightmares—"

"You think I don't know that? I can't sleep without seeing my best friend getting fucking *blown up*."

Rose flinched.

"Look, I should head out. I'll call you. Do you have to work today?" he asked.

"No. I'm going over to Heath's. He's picking me up."

"Good, good. I'll see you later."

He was so distracted that he only kissed her cheek before heading out, not even telling Callie goodbye like he usually did.

Rose rubbed her eyes, exhausted beyond measure. She'd lied about Heath coming by: she just hadn't wanted Seth to stick around because he felt guilty.

"Come on, girl," she said to Callie as she got Callie's leash, "let's go take a walk. Otherwise I'm going to lose my mind sitting around here."

Callie barked happily, and Rose was glad that at least somebody around here was happy for once.

WHEN SETH SCREWED up a table leg for the third time, Alan told him to take a break. "Otherwise I'm going to run out of wood," he said dryly.

Seth swore under his breath. He was too distracted to get any real work done; the usual peace he got from woodworking wasn't happening today.

He couldn't stop thinking about Rose's face when he'd told her he might say yes to a fourth tour. She'd been stricken, yet she hadn't told him to say no, either. *But what else can I do?* he thought rather desperately.

His mind whispered that he was just too scared to admit how much he cared for Rose—that he couldn't tell her that he loved her. Because the people he loved died, didn't they?

"You going to tell me what's going on or am I going to have to torture it out of you?" Alan joked. He handed Seth a mug of hot coffee. "I haven't seen you destroy a table leg like that since you were a kid."

Seth grunted. "Just a lot on my mind."

"No kidding. The missus got mad at me this morning because I'd forgotten to buy toilet paper. Like I'd remember her telling me that at seven yesterday morning when I don't get home until five! She told me to get out until I could get my head out of my ass." He whistled. "That woman has a temper, that's for sure."

"Did you buy the toilet paper?" Seth couldn't help but ask.

"Sure did. Rolls and rolls of it sitting in my trunk right now." Alan winked. "Because you gotta compromise to keep the peace. You can't keep fighting everyone and everything, son."

Seth wasn't sure how Alan buying toilet paper when his wife had asked him to do just that was compromising, but he just smiled, shaking his head.

Alan had been a father figure to him in a way, and Seth found himself wanting to tell him about Sergeant Loyd's offer. It wasn't as if his own father would be of any help: Dave Thornton had never been fond of his son's decision to join the Marines instead of doing something more prestigious. Like becoming a physician like himself and Harrison, or a lawyer. Or an investment banker or something like that. Something involving a suit, tie, and lots of money.

Alan listened without comment as Seth told him everything. Crossing his arms, Alan nodded and harrumphed a few times until Seth reached the end. Although he'd hardly mentioned Rose, apparently he'd said enough to convey that his feelings were more than just surface feelings.

"Here's the question," Alan said, "what do you *want?*"

"What do you mean?"

"Exactly what I said. Do you want to make sergeant? Go

back abroad to fight again? Or are you doing it because you're running from something—or someone?" Alan stroked his mustache. "Think about that, is what I'd say. It'd be one thing if you felt like this was the right path for you. It's another if you're doing it for stupid reasons altogether. And it sounds like you care about this girl a lot."

Seth shook his head. "I don't know what I feel."

"Yeah, you do. Don't be a dumbass, son." Alan slapped him on the shoulder. "Get your head out of the sand and figure it out. I have a feeling you know what the answer is; you just don't want to face it. We all get into that place. It's just a matter of how you get yourself out of it."

Seth was able to finish the table without destroying another leg, his mind focused on the task at hand.

On the drive home, his phone rang. "Hey, are you still coming to the thing tonight?" Lizzie asked him.

"The thing…"

"The Fourth of July party. You know, the one our parents put on just about every year…?"

He'd totally forgotten. Shit, today wasn't just Friday, but the Fourth of July, wasn't it? Seth grimaced. He *hated* fireworks. They just reminded him of the sound of bombs, and they inevitably went on all night long. Last year had been his first year back in the States for the Fourth of July, and he'd only made it through that night with a lot of booze and some earplugs. It hadn't helped, though, because the fireworks were close enough that that they shook the apartment.

"Yeah, I'll be there," he said, only so Lizzie wouldn't be suspicious.

"Bring Rose with you." Her tone was sly. "She can meet our parents finally."

That made Seth groan. "That's just evil, Lizard. She doesn't deserve that."

Lizzie laughed before they said goodbye. Seth hadn't planned on taking Rose to the party, mostly because his parents would descend on Rose like vultures. Then again, he wasn't about to leave her alone right now.

Rose agreed to come along after some persuasion. "Can I bring Callie?" she asked. "I hate to leave her alone with the fireworks going off."

Seth knew his mother hated dogs, so he said, "Yeah, sure."

They arrived at the Thornton mansion that sat in the hills overlooking Fair Haven later that evening. The sun wouldn't set until after nine o'clock, and the fireworks weren't scheduled until closer to ten thirty. Seth just prayed he could drink enough so nobody would notice his reaction to the fireworks.

Lizzie found him right away. She knew how the fireworks affected him, and she squeezed his arm. "I didn't want you to be alone," she explained. "Will you be okay?"

"I'm fine." He didn't want anyone hovering—especially not his sister.

Lizzie gave him an assessing look before turning to Rose. "It's so nice to see you! How are you?"

"I'm great. How are you? And Bea?"

Lizzie beamed. "Come and see for yourself. I think one of my brothers has snagged her. They act like such big strong men, but around their niece…"

Seth watched as Lizzie took Rose around, introducing her to anyone she hadn't already met. Not only were the Thorntons and their various significant others present, but a number of people from Fair Haven were there. The Thorntons never skimped on parties, that was for sure.

Some people Seth hadn't seen since before he'd enlisted came up to talk to him, including a few teachers he'd forgotten about from elementary and junior high school. It was a bit like a bizarre reunion of sorts, and Seth hadn't been prepared to answer the usual types of questions lobbed at him.

"What are you doing now?" and "What are your plans now that you're out of the Marines?"

He dodged those questions like bullets and found refuge with his brothers, who could at least be counted on not to ask the same damn questions over and over again.

"Seth!" Caleb gave him a hug. "Good, you came. We weren't sure you'd come. Hey, Harrison, when are the fireworks supposed to start again?"

"Ten forty-five."

"I'll tell Megan."

Caleb wandered off, leaving Seth with Harrison and soon thereafter, Mark. Caleb had always been the talker of the family, so without him, the brothers often fell into usually comfortable silences with each other.

"You brought Rose with you," Harrison finally said. "I'm glad she could come this time."

"I'd totally forgotten this was even happening," Seth admitted with a short laugh. "I've been preoccupied."

"We heard. Have you made a decision yet?" This from Mark.

Seth was about to ask how they knew, but then he rolled his eyes. "Can nothing in his family stay a secret?"

"No," said Mark and Harrison at the same time.

Seth told them what he'd told Alan earlier, except he made more of an effort to avoid saying anything about Rose. Now that both Harrison and Mark were happily married, they tended to act like everyone around them wanted to fall in love and get married and have families.

"There you are," Sara said as she approached the trio. "Your mom wanted to ask you where the champagne was stored."

Harrison rolled his eyes. "How should I know? I don't live here."

"Because you're the oldest." She smiled at Seth. "Long time no see. How are you?"

Seth could just make out a slight bump on Sara's figure, and when Harrison covered her belly with his palm and kissed the crown of her head, envy struck Seth like a lightning bolt.

He remembered Harrison as someone who didn't have time for relationships because he'd been too focused on his career as a pediatric oncologist. When Seth had first joined up, Harrison hadn't had a serious girlfriend in over two years. And Mark—Seth couldn't have been more shocked if someone had told him Mark had decided to dye his hair pink and become a pastry chef when he'd found out he'd fallen in love with Abby. Returning to so many of his siblings being happily married had been strange, like Seth had entered some alternate dimension.

The days of him and his brothers talking about all the beautiful women they met and enjoyed had vanished. Now it was marriage, babies, buying houses—adulthood in a nutshell.

Seth gave Sara a wan smile. "I'm fine. How are you?"

After that, Seth mostly listened as everyone talked about their lives, their jobs, the usual types of things. Harrison and Sara were debating whether or not they wanted to find out the gender of their baby, while Mark and Abby were enjoying the latest foal that had been born on Mark's ranch.

Rose found him after a while, looking happy but a little out of her element.

"Where's Lizzie?" he asked her. He frowned. "She didn't abandon you, did she?"

"No, she just had to go nurse Bea. Everyone has been perfectly nice."

"Have you met my mother?"

She laughed. "Not yet. She's been too busy, I guess."

Lisa Thornton found them both soon thereafter. With her icy beauty and imperious stare, Lisa inspired admiration and fear in everyone she met. Her adult children still found her formidable.

"Seth, there you are. I haven't seen you in ages," Lisa admonished as she hugged him. "What have you been doing with yourself?"

"Sorry, Mom. I've meant to stop by," he lied. He gestured toward Rose. "Have you met Rose DiMarco? She's Heath's younger sister."

Lisa held out a hand that had a large diamond ring on her finger. "Rose, it's so nice to meet you. You live next door to my son?"

"That's right," Rose said as she took Lisa's hand. "I moved in about a month ago."

"Excellent. Well, I hope you two enjoy yourselves. I have to find your father." She patted Seth on the arm and hurried off.

Seth stared after Lisa, nonplussed. "That was—"

"Anticlimactic?" Rose supplied.

They both looked at each other and laughed. Maybe the rumors about Lisa not being quite as intense were true.

Seth and Rose drank and talked, and Rose lit sparklers

with Sara's son, James, before the fireworks show. Now eight years old, James was bright and growing like a weed. Although Harrison was his stepfather, he'd become more of a father to James since his marriage to Sara. James even called him Dad, despite his real father's protests.

"You have to do it like this," James said, demonstrating for Rose. "Right. Watch me, okay?"

Rose stood and watched, her expression serious, as James showed her the proper way to make swirls with the sparkler. James was so intent that he didn't even notice Rose grinning at Seth.

*God, I love her*, Seth thought, realizing he was smiling like a fool right now. As he watched her play with James, the two of them making figure eights that seemed to be burned into the very air, he almost blurted out the words right then. He loved her so much it hurt.

When James ran off to get a hot dog, Seth almost took her into a private corner to tell her. But then Dave Thornton got up and yelled, "The fireworks are starting in five minutes! Get to your places, everyone!"

Seth froze, but with the crowd moving to get the best spots, Rose didn't notice. They found themselves next to Megan and Caleb, everyone talking and laughing before the show began. Since the Thorntons were outside the city limits, they were able to do their own show—and even if anyone objected, they knew too many people in town to get them-selves slapped with a fine.

Seth gritted his teeth, steeling himself. When the first fire-work went off, he closed his eyes.

At first, he thought he was fine. He wasn't shaking, and he knew where he was. He felt Rose against him, and he heard her gasps at the bright colors and explosions overhead.

But as the fireworks went on and on, seemingly without end, he realized he *was* shaking. He was afraid he was going to throw up. When a firework burst multiple times in a row, crackling like gunfire, he pushed whoever was behind him aside. He couldn't breathe; he gasped for air.

Finally, he broke free of the crowd, and he didn't even see where he was going: he just ran until he collapsed onto his knees, his hands over his ears as the explosions went on and on.

# CHAPTER SEVENTEEN

One moment Seth was next to her watching the fireworks, the next he was pushing his way through the crowd. He disappeared from her line of sight for a moment.

"What's wrong?" Caleb yelled over the latest firework explosion.

"I don't know! I need to go after him."

Rose ducked under someone's arm and headed toward the Thornton house. She saw a door close, and she went inside the house, which was mostly dark except for a dim light from the hallway. She'd gone through a back door that led into a mudroom. She waited a moment and then heard footsteps. She ran after the sound.

She discovered Seth in a room upstairs, his head in his hands. She glanced at the decor and realized that this must have been his childhood room: there were posters of rock bands on the walls, a giant but old stereo on a table near the bed, and a scattering of rudimentary wooden figurines. She almost smiled when she saw the desktop computer still sitting on the desk.

"Seth." He didn't respond, and she sat down next to him on the bed, careful not to startle him. "Seth, it's me. It's Rose."

He just shook his head. When a firework went off, he flinched, the sound echoing through the house. Rose could even feel the walls shake from the blast.

Seth seemed to close further in on himself, like he could protect himself from the thoughts ricocheting in his mind. Rose's heart shattered as she watched him.

"Seth," she said again. She touched his arm, but he wrenched away from her.

"Go. Away." His voice was raspy and harsh, and she barely recognized the sound. "Go away."

"I'm not leaving you like this. I'll stay for as long as it takes."

He didn't answer.

The grand finale of the fireworks was the worst: the explosion and the *pat-pat-pat* continued on and on, and with each sound, Seth shuddered.

"I'm here," she said, because she didn't know what else to do. "I'm here. It's me. You're safe. Can you hear me?"

When the fireworks ended, Rose breathed a sigh of relief. After what seemed an eternity, Seth began to uncurl himself, and when she saw his expression, she almost cried. He looked battered and drained and so vulnerable she wanted to take away all of his pain.

She understood that kind of pain all too well, and she never wanted someone she loved to know what it felt like.

She reached out and put a hand on his arm. A second later, Rose found herself pushed away so hard that she fell onto the floor as Seth wrenched himself away from her. Jumping up, he yelled, "Don't fucking touch me!"

Rose stared up at him. In that moment, she knew that he didn't know where he was. Her heart pounding, she whispered, "I'm sorry. I won't touch you again."

"Can't fucking *touch* me," he muttered. He tugged at his hair, his eyes wild, and Rose just waited, praying he'd return to himself.

When he did, he stared at her in shock. Then his face twisted with horror.

"Rose—goddamn. Are you okay?" He helped her up, and she felt him tremble. "Did I hurt you?"

"No, no, you just startled me. I'm fine. Seth, do you know where you are?"

He was so stricken that he turned away from her. "I could've hurt you," he said, his voice full of despair. "You should leave."

"I'm not leaving you now. You had an episode. Do you want to go to the hospital?"

"No!" He whirled on her. Trying to calm himself, he said more quietly, "No. I'll be fine. I just need to sit for a while in silence."

"Then I'll sit with you."

He nodded, and they sat back down on the bed. Rose didn't touch him, no matter how much she wanted to.

They didn't have long to sit in silence. The door burst open, and in came what seemed like the entire Thornton family.

"We heard a shout. Jesus, what happened?" Caleb demanded.

After him followed Lizzie, Harrison, and then Lisa.

"Seth, Caleb said you left the fireworks show," Lizzie said

as she sat down in a chair next to him. "Can you talk? You're scaring me."

Lisa's expression was even more stricken than Seth's had been moments earlier. To Rose's shock, she saw tears on Lisa's face.

"I didn't know," Lisa whispered. When Seth didn't respond, she spoke to Rose. "I didn't know. I would never have had the fireworks. He never said a word. He said he was fine…"

Rose stood and took Lisa's hand, squeezing it. Lisa began to cry harder, and she turned away, obviously embarrassed by this onslaught of emotion.

"Seth, talk to me." Harrison kneeled in front of his younger brother. "What happened? Can you tell me?"

Seth stood up again, and Harrison almost fell over. It would've been comical if everyone weren't so worried.

"Will you all just. Get. OUT!" Seth shouted the last two words until everyone winced. "GET. OUT!"

"Everyone needs to leave," Abby said as she bustled inside.

Rose vaguely remembered being told that Abby was an ER nurse, and based on her current demeanor, Rose could see why. Within moments, Abby had gotten everyone—except Rose—to leave so she could look over Seth.

Abby was able to piece together an explanation from both Rose and Seth, and after Seth declined going to the hospital a second time, Abby took Rose aside.

"He needs to go home and rest. If anything else happens, though, take him straight to the ER, got it?"

Rose nodded, almost numb at this point. "Got it."

Rose collected Callie, who'd stayed by James's side and who seemed the most disappointed to be leaving early.

Rose barely remembered driving Seth back to their apartments. She declined to tell anyone her driver's license had expired ages ago.

Sensing that her two favorite humans were upset, Callie laid her head, chin down, on the center console. Periodically, Rose would scratch her behind the ears, and she could hear Callie's tail thump against the backseats.

"I'm staying with you," Rose said as Seth opened his front door.

He didn't protest, but he didn't seem to hear her, either. He mumbled something about taking a shower. Rose took Callie for a quick walk before having her settle down on some blankets in the living room.

"Are you hungry?" she asked Seth when he emerged from his bedroom. "I could make us something."

He shook his head. "You should go home," he said. "You don't need to stay here."

"Of course I do. Seth, what happened tonight—"

"I don't want to talk about it. It happened, whatever. I'll get over it."

He collapsed onto his couch and closed his eyes. Rose finally sat next to him, still afraid to touch him.

"Did I hurt you?" He opened his eyes; his gaze was clear but stark.

"No. It was an accident. You didn't know where you were."

"Didn't I? All I could hear were the bombs—fireworks—and I just lost my fucking mind." He smiled grimly. "Didn't I say I didn't want to talk about it?"

After a long moment, he sighed. "You should go, Rose."

"And leave you alone right now? No way." She glared at him. "So stop telling me to leave already."

SETH ALMOST LAUGHED at Rose's obstinate expression. Of course she wouldn't leave, she was as stubborn as anyone he knew. Maybe even more stubborn than Lizzie, which was saying something.

His head pounded, and he wished he could drink until he blacked out. Too bad he only had a few beers in his fridge. Maybe he could go to the corner store…

He doubted alcohol could banish the thoughts replaying over and over in his mind: the sound of the fireworks; the smell of blood filling his nostrils; the heat of sand; the screams. Past and present had blurred until he couldn't decipher which was which. He'd never lost himself so completely before, and God Almighty, it terrified him.

And then he'd knocked Rose to the floor without even knowing he was doing it.

She wasn't hurt, thank God, but he felt guilty anyway. He could've hurt her. What if he'd pushed her hard enough that she struck her head on something? Horror congealed in his gut.

He might not have hurt her tonight, but that didn't mean he wouldn't hurt her later. He'd been deceiving himself, thinking he could make a life for himself here. He was good for nothing but being a soldier. Without the Marines, he was just a shell of a man, too terrified to enjoy a damn fireworks show on the Fourth of July.

"I'm not the one running, Rose. You are."

"Maybe I am running. But at least it's not toward my own death."

The anger burst inside him like the fireworks from that evening. It spiked his blood, and with a quick grab, he yanked Rose into his arms. She gasped.

"You don't know what you're talking about. You have no idea."

Her smile was so sad right then. "Don't I?"

They stared at each other, their chests sawing for breath. The moment heated, expanded, until the tension made him tremble. He dipped his head toward her, needing her taste, her touch, but she pushed at his chest.

"Let me go."

He hesitated. Then he freed her from his embrace.

"I'm going, just like you wanted. And I won't be back."

When she slammed the door behind her, he didn't even flinch.

## CHAPTER EIGHTEEN

Rose entered her own apartment and stood in the middle of her living room. Her brain couldn't compute what had just happened. She stared at the dirty dishes currently sitting in the sink, the mug on the coffee table where she'd left it this morning. It had seemed ages ago, drinking from the mug.

Callie whined and sat next to Rose. She whined again, but Rose didn't respond.

It was over. After everything that had happened to her, she'd fallen in love with a man who didn't want to fight for that love. He wanted to let himself fall deeper into his own doom, and she could do nothing about it.

A stray firework exploded some miles away; she flinched. She waited for a second one, and she breathed a sigh of relief when that seemed to be the only one.

She washed the dishes that had been sitting in the sink all day. She washed her face, brushed her teeth, got dressed for bed. Pulling out the futon, she realized that her pillow smelled like Seth. Exchanging it for another pillow, she almost screamed—all of her pillows smelled like him.

She rolled up a blanket and used that as a pillow instead. She tried to close her eyes and sleep, but it was pointless. Her mind wouldn't settle. Over and over, she saw Seth tell her to go, tell her not to love him.

Rose squeezed her eyes shut. She heard someone gasping, like through a tunnel, only to realize a long moment later that it was her. She clapped a hand over her mouth to stifle the sound. She refused to let Seth know how much he'd hurt her.

*Sleep, sleep, sleep,* she chanted inwardly. *If I can't sleep, then I can't stop thinking about what happened.*

Yet her mind wouldn't let any of it go. She went over every word, every expression, everything conveyed tonight. She felt like she was going to choke, and she finally sat up, coughing and panting. Tears burned her eyelids. That familiar friend—panic—climbed up her throat and threatened to strangle her.

"Oh God, oh God, oh God," she muttered. She put her head in her hands. Rocking back and forth, she chewed on the inside of her cheek to muffle the sounds of her sobs, but after a while, she couldn't keep them contained anymore. Grabbing the rolled-up blanket, she buried her face in it and cried until her eyes were swollen and her head pounded.

She cried until she could barely rise to go the bathroom. When she saw her reflection in the mirror, she instantly switched off the light, but that one glimpse had shown her that she looked like she'd been dragged to hell and back again.

Rose returned to the futon and curled up into a ball. Stray tears leaked from her eyes, and she was too tired to wipe them away. Callie lay on the floor next to her the entire time, full of canine concern.

"I love him," she whispered. "I still love him."

This hurt more than what Johnny had done to her because she knew Seth cared for her. Loved her, even. Yet he'd turned his back on her when she'd made herself vulnerable and confessed her feelings. Even worse was knowing that he was punishing himself for losing Max. He'd accused her of being a coward, but if anyone was a coward, it was Seth.

Everything—Johnny, the money, the threats—seemed unimportant. She couldn't bring herself to care. She knew she was going to meet Johnny tomorrow—or was it already today?—at the Sanditon Pass. She'd already set her alarm to get up early to catch the bus. But when before she would've been a bundle of nerves, now she was numb.

She began to fall asleep, but then she felt something solid drop into the palm of her hand. She opened her eyes to see that Callie had brought her that damn hummingbird figurine that Seth had let her keep. The tears sprang up again, and she burst into a second bout of tears. She clutched the figurine to her heart until she was so exhausted from crying that she finally went to sleep.

It was early afternoon by the time Rose arrived in the last town before you hiked up to the Sanditon Pass. As the bus traveled closer and closer to her destination, she began to feel the nerves again. The money in her jacket pocket, along with her gun, seemed inordinately heavy.

She took a deep breath, glanced at the directions Johnny had given her, and started walking.

It was about two miles into a wooded area, bursting with evergreens and wildflowers. The grass whistled in the breeze, dry and yellow from the summer dry spell, and if Rose weren't walking to what she knew was her certain doom, she might have enjoyed the walk. When a butterfly fluttered past her, she had to stifle a hysterical laugh.

She'd done as Johnny had asked her: she hadn't told anyone where she was going—at least not yet. She checked her phone to make sure she still had cell service, and she sent off a quick text to Heath. *I'm at Sanditon Pass* was all she wrote. By the time Heath saw the text, she'd be without service.

At least this way, her brother could find her if she didn't come back.

Fear crawled up her spine, and she sent up a silent prayer to whoever was listening that she would get out of this alive. If she could just persuade Johnny to take the money…

She arrived at a cabin around a long bend, and it looked so idyllic that Rose was afraid she'd taken a wrong turn. Then she saw Johnny's car before Johnny himself walked outside.

"You're here!" he said. He had a cigarette in his hand as he embraced her. "I thought you'd never come."

The hug lingered, and Rose gritted her teeth to keep herself from wrenching away. Slithers of disgust ran up and down her body from his mere proximity. He smiled down at her, his teeth flashing in the bright sunshine.

"Let's go inside. Are you hungry? It's almost lunch." He acted like this was some bizarre picnic, and Rose wanted to strangle him.

"I'm not going inside with you." She pulled out the envelope of cash and held it out. "Here's your money: every cent is there, including interest. Now leave me and my family alone. We're done."

Johnny looked at the money like she'd tried to give him a dead frog. "Didn't I say I didn't want your money?"

"I'm paying you back. Take it."

He didn't speak for a long moment. Finally, he took the money, and Rose breathed a deep sigh of relief.

Until she saw the smile forming on Johnny's face.

"Rosie, Rosie, Rosie. So sweet and naïve still. You amaze me. Did you really think you could pay me off and I'd let you go?" He moved so close to her that she felt his clove-scented breath on her face. "There's no way in hell you're going home now," he whispered.

"You have your money. What else do you want?"

He touched her cheek, and this time, she did flinch.

"Now, are you going to come inside, or am I going to have to persuade you to?"

The second he stepped away, she pulled out her gun, aiming it straight at his heart like she'd done at the park weeks ago.

"I'm not going anywhere with you. Either let me leave, or I'll shoot you." She knew that this time, she wouldn't even hesitate.

He shrugged. "Do it. Shoot me. But I wouldn't recommend it."

Rose had her finger on the trigger now. The sun beat down on her neck, sweat breaking out on her forehead. Licking her lips, she rasped, "Let me go, Johnny."

"You can leave if you want, but like I said: there will be

consequences." He smiled again as he reached inside his pocket for something.

Rose expected a gun, but when he pulled out what looked like a dark ribbon, she hesitated. It wasn't a ribbon, though: it was a lock of hair.

"Just so you know, we have one of your friends here. What was her name? Jenny? Julie? Jubilee!" He laughed. "Interesting name. I wonder if it's a family name."

Rose felt the blood drain from her face as she stared at that long strand of dark hair, the same color as Seth's. Only Jubilee had hair that long. Her heart stuttered as the lock blew in the breeze, taunting her.

Oh God, not Jubilee. Why Jubilee? She was innocent in all of this. Rose struggled to understand why Johnny would choose her, but to him, any person who knew Rose could be used against her. If he had hurt her, or God forbid, raped her—

She closed her eyes for a split second. She couldn't give into panic, that was what Johnny wanted.

"So, you have two choices," Johnny said conversationally as he swung the lock back and forth. "You can leave and we'll kill your friend. Or, you can come with me, and we'll let her go."

Rose took her finger from the trigger. "You swear to let Jubilee go?"

"Of course. I always keep my promises."

A bird cawed in a tree nearby. Johnny waited, his eyebrows slightly raised. The lock of hair looked like a tiny noose now.

When she lowered her gun, putting the safety back on, Johnny laughed. Then before Rose could react, Johnny slapped her—hard—the gun skittering across the ground. She staggered as Johnny grabbed her forearm, his fingers digging into her skin.

"You've made the right choice, my dear," he said as he dragged her into the cabin.

She struggled, trying to free herself from his grip, but he only grabbed her by the hair and shook her.

"Behave yourself." He pulled her head back, exposing her throat. "Or your little friend is going to have a very bad time."

Johnny took her to a bedroom in the back of the cabin. There was no furniture to speak of. It was a prison cell.

"Where's Jubilee?" Rose demanded. "If you've hurt her, I'll kill you. I swear it."

"Where's Jubilee? Funny you should ask that." He turned his brightest smile on her—so bright that she almost had to close her eyes. "I hate to say this, but I lied."

She blinked. "What?"

"I lied. We don't have the girl. You gave yourself up for no reason."

At her stricken expression, he laughed. Then he slammed the door and locked it, leaving her to scream at him from inside her makeshift cell.

"Seth, it's Jubilee. Open up. I have cupcakes."

Seth heard Jubilee's voice and winced. What time was it? He groaned when he saw it was almost noon. He couldn't remember when he'd fallen asleep last night after…everything.

Even the mention of cupcakes from The Rise and Shine wasn't enough of a temptation to rouse him from his bed.

"I'm sleeping!" he yelled and burrowed below the covers.

"I'm not leaving until you open the door. Or I'll just call Mom and have her come by—"

Seth opened the door to see his little sister beaming up at him.

"You're evil," he said as she came inside.

"No, just effective. Here, I brought one of each flavor. I thought you'd need it." She looked at him and sighed. "Are you okay?"

What a question! No, he wasn't okay. He'd told Rose he couldn't love her and that they were over. He was going to accept Sergeant Loyd's offer and leave for another tour in the fall.

All in all, he was a damn wreck.

"Fine," he said as he plucked a chocolate cupcake from the platter. It tasted like sand in his mouth, but he needed to eat something. "You didn't have to come by."

"I wanted to. I had the day off, and Lizzie texted me... I heard about what happened last night. Do you want to talk about it?"

It struck him then that his little sister wasn't a child anymore. She'd grown up while he'd been away fighting. It depressed him. What had happened to the sweet girl who'd hung onto his every word? Who'd had to be protected and coddled because she'd suffered from leukemia twice in her short life?

"I don't want to talk about it." At her sad expression, he sighed. "You can sit with me, though. Tell me what's going on with you."

Jubilee sensed that he wanted peace and quiet, though, and she didn't chatter his ear off. The younger Jubilee would've taken the opportunity to tell him *everything*, but not this Jubilee. She had a maturity to her that Seth could barely reconcile with the girl he'd known.

"Do you love her?" Jubilee asked suddenly.

He didn't need to ask who she meant. "Yes. But it doesn't matter."

"Of course it matters. Have you told her how you feel? Because she feels the same."

He narrowed his eyes. "How do *you* know?"

"You know, when you've been kept in a bubble your entire life, you tend to pay attention to other people. You don't have any interesting stories about yourself, so you have to discover someone else's." Her smile was bittersweet. "Point being, I saw the way she looked at you at the party last night. It was obvious to anyone with working eyeballs."

That made him groan. He dropped his face into his hands. "I've fucked it all up, Jubi."

"Come on, tell me. I've seen Harrison, Caleb, and Mark all screw up with their soulmates and look at them now. They figured it out."

*That doesn't mean I will.*

He told her about Sergeant Loyd's offer, about how last night had made him sure it was the right decision. He told her about his fight with Rose, how things had fallen apart. He didn't tell her about Johnny, although the thought of what Rose had gone through—and the fact that he'd added to her burden—only made him feel worse.

He needed to talk to her. He couldn't be the right guy for her, but he'd made her a promise to keep her safe.

"Love sucks," Jubilee said, "but it also makes you a better

person. I've seen how you are around Rose. We all have. It's like you've come back to yourself."

"I've always been myself."

She shook her head. "When you came back last year…you weren't the older brother I'd known. I knew you wouldn't be— it'd been so long since you'd really been home. But sometimes I couldn't find that person in you still. Does that make sense?"

"You're not the little girl I left behind, either."

"I hope not. I haven't been a little girl in a long time."

Looking at Jubilee, he knew she spoke the truth. He'd returned to Fair Haven a shell of a man, but Rose? Rose had awoken a purpose within him, and she'd loved him despite everything he'd done. He swallowed, a lump in his throat.

*Maybe I can make a life here. Maybe I can be the man Rose thinks I am.*

It was a heady thought, and one he wanted to make happen more than he'd ever wanted anything.

"You'll find a way. Just tell Rose you're sorry."

He smiled. "How do you know it's my fault?"

"It's always the guy's fault."

He challenged that, and they bickered like siblings until they were both laughing.

"How do you know so much about love?" Seth couldn't help but ask. He watched Jubilee's cheeks turn red. "Is there somebody you like?"

"I'm not telling you that."

"Hey, that's not fair. I told you everything."

Jubilee opened her mouth to reply when someone banged on the front door. They both jumped at the sound.

"Seth! Open up! It's Heath! Rose is missing."

Seth wrenched open the door to see a red-faced, panting Heath, his eyes wild with panic.

"It's Rose," he said again. "She's not answering her phone, she isn't home, and she sent me this text." He showed Seth his phone, which had a single text from Rose: *I'm at Sanditon Pass.*

"Why the fuck would she go there…?"

The two men both stared at each other when they realized the exact reason why. The blood drained from Seth's face.

*"Johnny."*

"What is it? What's happened?" Jubilee took in their faces and turned pale. "You guys are scaring me."

"Jubi, call Caleb. Tell him I need him to get a team to go up to Sanditon Pass."

She frowned, but at his determined expression, she didn't balk. And Seth didn't have time to explain.

Rose was in danger. Had Johnny taken her? His mind whirled, but his soldier's training kept him calm. After he gathered his gun and enough bullets for an hours-long gunfight, he headed out.

"Wait!" Heath grabbed his arm. "I'm coming with you."

"Stay here. Find Caleb, and take Jubi with you. She can help."

Heath looked like he wanted to protest, but sensing he would lose that battle, he nodded tightly.

"Go get my sister, Thornton," he said, his eyes flashing. "Otherwise I'll find you and shoot you myself."

"If I don't find her, I'll be begging you to shoot me."

# CHAPTER NINETEEN

After Johnny left her, Rose took in the room, looking for any means of escape. There was no furniture, nothing to use as a weapon to get the zip ties loose. Rose struggled for a while, until she realized all she was doing was hurting herself in the process.

She forced herself to stay calm. She'd texted Heath her location, and she knew her brother would move heaven and earth to find her. Closing her eyes, she breathed deeply, in and out.

What would Seth do? Sitting in this prison cell, tied up and terrified, she felt all of her feelings of anger and grief toward Seth melt away. She wanted to see him one last time because no matter what, she loved him. What if she never got to tell him how much she loved him again?

She choked back a sob at that thought. She couldn't devolve into panic, or she would never get out of this alive.

Johnny had used zip ties on her wrists and her ankles, tying each ankle to the chair itself. Years ago, she'd taken a brief self-defense class, and she forced herself to remember what they'd learned about getting out of zip ties. Her mind was so dizzy with fear, though, that it took her some time to calm herself enough to think clearly.

*Think. Don't let him win like this, Rose.*

She remembered practicing, how it had taken her a bunch of tries, but she'd finally broken free of the zip-ties during the class. Thinking back to that experience, she leaned down and took the free end of the zip tie and bit down to tighten it as much as she could around her wrists.

Then she lifted her hands up and brought them down quickly against her stomach.

Nothing. The zip tie hadn't budged.

She tightened it again with her teeth and when she brought her hands down, she did it with more force, to the point that she almost tipped herself over. She was able to steady herself, but it had been a close call.

"One more try. You can do this," she muttered to herself.

*Tighten; lift your arms; bring them down and flare your shoulders to break the zip tie.*

With a gasp, she felt the zip tie break. It fell into her lap, and within moments, she had gotten herself free from the chair.

She wished Seth could see her. She smiled, thinking about how he'd react when she told him how she'd gotten free.

She didn't move toward the window just yet. Listening, she could hear Johnny talking to somebody further inside the cabin, and she heard booted footsteps.

If she waited too long, he would find her and she'd never escape.

The window, to her relief, was easily pushed open. She had to rip through the screen, which took longer than she would've anticipated. Her palms became sweaty when she finally had a hole big enough to climb through.

"Where do you think you're going?" Johnny grabbed her hair and dragged her back into the room.

Rose screamed, twisting in his grip. She freed herself, only to have him grab her wrists and whirl her around so her back was against his front.

"Bad girls who try to escape get punished," he hissed into her ear. He wrenched her arms back until she cried out in pain.

"Fuck you, Johnny. You'll pay for this. My brother and Seth will save me—"

He yanked her arms back until Rose was afraid he'd dislocate her shoulder. She panted, trying to keep the panic at bay, but when Johnny began to creep a hand up her bare back, she couldn't stop herself from trying to get away.

She was like a cat, all limbs and claws, and she pushed and struggled against Johnny. When she was able to stomp on his instep, he swore and let her go.

"Don't touch me!" She fought him, not caring where she clawed and hit him. She wouldn't let him hurt her again: she'd die trying to escape from him.

"Stop this! Goddammit, Rosie, you're pissing me off—"

At this point, they'd moved nearer to the abandoned chair, and before Johnny could react, she'd grabbed the chair and bashed him over the head with it. He groaned and collapsed at her feet.

Panting, she wondered if she'd killed him. Bending down, she heard him make a noise, and he was still breathing. She grimaced. She was considering finishing the job when she heard footsteps. She needed to get out of here.

Climbing out of the window, Rose sprinted into the woods, running parallel to the path that had taken her to the cabin. She ran for she didn't know how long, but her lungs ached and her breath sawed from her throat.

When she saw a figure emerge from behind a tree, she was about to scream when a hand clapped over her mouth.

"It's Seth," the voice said as she continued to struggle. "Hummingbird, it's me. You're safe."

It took her a moment to understand what he was saying, to believe that this wasn't some trick. Then all of the fight went out of her, and she collapsed against him.

"Rose," Seth said, and she turned in his arms and hugged him so hard he laughed a little. "Are you okay? Did that bastard hurt you? Talk to me. Jesus Christ, *Rose*."

She looked up, and she saw his face darken when he noticed the bruise on her cheek.

"That piece of shit. I'll kill him." His eyes roved over her, drinking her in. "Did he hurt you?" He swallowed, stricken.

She shook her head. "I got away. I hit him with a chair." She breathed in his scent and allowed herself a moment to feel safe.

"We need to get out of here," she said. "Johnny will be coming for me. He has men, too. I don't know how many." Then, remembering, she clutched his shirt: "Jubilee! Do you know where she is?"

Seth frowned. "Jubi? She was with me until Heath came to tell me you were missing."

That made Rose sag with relief, and she almost started sobbing. Gathering her composure, she whispered, "He lied. Thank God."

"I have no idea what you're talking about." He kissed her

forehead and smoothed her hair back from her face. "You need to keep running. Caleb and his guys are on their way, and you'll meet up with them. I'll catch up with you."

"No, Seth, I'm not leaving you again." Her voice trembled as she saw the determination in his face.

"I'm not going to let Johnny get away again." He cupped her cheek. "I love you, Rose. I'm sorry I was too much of a coward to tell you earlier."

A sob escaped before she kissed him. He responded with a groan and then pushed her away.

"Go, Rose. Now."

"Isn't this lovely?" Johnny's voice echoed through the woods. He and four other guys emerged and quickly encircled Rose and Seth.

Johnny had a huge bruise forming on his temple, which made Rose inordinately proud. She stood next to Seth and tipped up her chin.

"Have a nice nap, Johnny?" she called.

His face turned red, and she laughed at him. When he wanted to lunge at her, one of Johnny's guys stopped him. Seth moved her so she stood behind him, although they had two guys with their guns pointed at their back, and two guys with their guns pointed at their fronts.

In a word, they were trapped. And Johnny smiled when they realized that.

SETH TOOK IN THE SITUATION, keeping Rose close to his side. He cursed himself for not making her run the second he'd found her, but he'd been so relieved at seeing her that he couldn't think like a soldier. He could only react like a man who'd been reunited with the love of his life.

Seth knew what he had to do, and it could very well get him killed. If it would save Rose, it would be worth it. Leaning down, he whispered in her ear, "I'm going to distract Johnny. Run the second the guys behind us aren't looking."

She nodded. She didn't tell him not to do it, although he saw it in her eyes.

"I love you," she whispered back. "Don't be an idiot."

That made his lips quirk. He moved his arm away from Rose's waist and then put enough space between them that if Johnny's guys shot at him, he wasn't close enough to endanger Rose. Hopefully, at least.

Seth had his own gun, but even he couldn't take out five men at once without endangering Rose in the process. If he could just get her out of here…

"How does it make you feel that Rose doesn't want you?" Seth taunted. "She hates you so much that she left you for dead and escaped to find me."

Johnny's face creased with anger, and Seth couldn't help but enjoy himself.

"You're a bastard, the worst kind of man. You force yourself on women and abuse them because you have no honor." Seth sneered as he moved further away from Rose. "Is this how you get a woman to be with you? You're pathetic. The most pathetic piece of shit I've ever met, and I've met a lot of people."

Johnny's face darkened until it was bright red, and Seth could make out a vein pulsing in his forehead. One of Johnny's men barked, "Shut up already. Unless you want to be shot."

Seth put up his hands. "Just pointing out the obvious. That your guy is a coward. What does it feel like, taking commands from a guy who's so pathetic that women literally run away from him? I'm not sure that's the guy I'd be taking orders from."

"Shut the fuck up!" Johnny yelled, advancing on Seth. "You don't know what the fuck you're talking about."

When Johnny launched himself at Seth, Seth yelled, "Run!"

He heard someone running into the brush, and when he saw that Rose was gone, he exulted. Johnny grabbed ahold of Seth's shirt and was about to slam his head into the ground when Seth pushed Johnny over, punching him in the face.

Johnny swore. Seth heard Johnny's guys move closer, but they couldn't get a shot at him without potentially killing Johnny.

He and Johnny rolled, punching where they could. Johnny got a fist to Seth's gut, knocking the wind from him. Seth got Johnny into a headlock, pressing on his throat.

When one of Johnny's guys was about to pull the trigger, Seth said, "Try that and I'll break his neck."

The man hesitated, and then he motioned for them all to put down their guns. Seth was halfway tempted to break Johnny's neck anyway; he deserved worse.

But Johnny wasn't about to give up yet. He somehow managed to reach near his knee and pull out a knife. He swiped it at Seth's face, forcing Seth to let him go.

Johnny got to his feet. "Shoot him!" he screamed.

Seth saw one of the men lift his gun again, and so he launched himself straight at Johnny. The sound of a gunshot exploded around him, momentarily deafening him. But all he could think of was getting that knife away from Johnny. They rolled in the dirt, grappling and punching. Johnny sliced at Seth and cut him across his left bicep.

Seth hissed in pain. He felt blood dripping down his arm, but it only gave him more of a reason to keep fighting.

But Johnny was a dirty fighter: he kneed Seth in the groin and then had the knife pressed to Seth's throat.

He looked down at Seth with sheer glee. "Now I get to kill you. I'll do it slowly, though, because you've made me so angry." He pressed the knife into Seth's skin, creating a thin line of blood. "And Rose will be mine."

*Over my dead body.* Seth grabbed the knife by its blade, yelling at the pain at his hand, but Johnny was so surprised that Seth was able to wrench it away from him and toss it far into the woods.

"Goddamn you!" Johnny screamed.

He was about to launch himself at Seth again when they heard, "Police! Put your weapons down and your hands up!"

Everyone froze, and then, like something out of a dream, Caleb and six other police officers surrounded them.

"Put your weapons down!" Caleb yelled. His gun was leveled at Johnny. "Otherwise we have orders to shoot to kill."

Johnny's men dropped their guns without another word, while Johnny just smiled. He reached into his pocket and pulled out his gun, dropping it at his feet.

"I surrender," he said, his tone disgusted.

The police converged on the group, putting Johnny and his guys in handcuffs. Seth clutched his hand to his chest as he rose from the ground.

"Seth, let's get you out of here." Caleb helped him up. He

winced when he saw Seth's injuries. "Can you walk? The ambulance isn't far from here."

Seth nodded. "I'm fine. It's just my hand." He noticed the red stain on his sleeve and added, "And my arm, I guess."

"Jesus Christ, Seth, you crazy asshole." Caleb pulled him into a bear hug, which Seth tried to reciprocate despite all the bleeding.

"Where's Rose? Did she find you?"

"I'm right here."

Seth looked over Caleb's shoulder, and then Rose was running into his arms. He pulled her into an embrace, spinning her around. He kissed her so hard that she yelped, but she didn't protest. God, he loved her. How could he have ever thought he'd leave her?

"Are you okay? God, Rose, it was so close—"

"Shh, I'm fine. Better than you." She ripped at her t-shirt and made a makeshift bandage for his hand. Tying it, she said, "You idiot. What were you thinking?"

He dropped his forehead to rest against hers. "I was thinking that as long as you were safe, I didn't care what happened."

"Well, I care what happens to you. And you're never doing something so moronic ever again."

That made him smile. "Of course, princess," he said, unable to help himself from using his original nickname for her.

She sniffed. "And don't you forget it."

CHAPTER TWENTY

It was nearly dawn by the time Rose and Seth returned to Seth's apartment. He had to get stitches in his hand, his bicep and throat were bandaged , and after long interviews with the cops, they were allowed to go home. Johnny and his gang would remain in jail for the time being.

Heath had taken Callie for the day, and when they'd all met up at the hospital, he'd returned her with a shake of his head.

"She wouldn't calm down all day," he'd reported as Callie cavorted around Rose in excitement. "I think she missed you."

Rose had almost cried at seeing Callie again. Burying her face in the dog's fur, she'd had to gather her composure to thank her brother for everything.

Now in Seth's apartment, they both collapsed onto Seth's bed, Callie lying at the foot of the bed. Seth winced when he rolled onto his side.

"How's your hand?" Rose asked as she curled next to him.

"Fine. I think they gave me enough painkillers to sedate an elephant."

"Good. Then if you annoy me, I'll put some into your food as revenge."

He laughed. "I guess I'd deserve it." His expression sobered; he touched her cheek that was now black and blue. "I've thought about what you said, before this happened."

"No, you don't have to—"

He interrupted her. "No, I want to. You said I was being a coward, and you were right. I was going to take Sergeant Loyd's offer because I thought there was nothing else for me here. Except I was wrong." He stroked her hair, his touch so gentle it made Rose want to cry all over again. "I have *you*. You're my everything, Rose."

Her heart expanded; she struggled to find the right words. "You're not going, then?" she whispered.

"No. If the Marines had something else for me, that'd be one thing. But I'm not going on another tour."

Rose hadn't cried all day—not really—but for some reason, this unleashed a flood of tears. Sobbing, she covered her face with her hands. She heard Seth saying something in soothing tones. He kissed her forehead.

"Jesus, don't cry, I can't stand it. Now you're making me wonder if you're sad I'm not going."

That made her cry harder. "You're so *stupid*. I thought everything was over between us, and then today you could've died—"

He moved her hands away from her face, but she could barely see through the tears.

"You could've died, too. Realizing you were missing, that Johnny had you... I was never so afraid as I was in that moment."

"I'm sorry. I should've told you." She wiped her eyes, sniffling. "I thought I could end it myself. I wanted to prove to myself that I could. Or that I just didn't care anymore. I don't know."

"Promise me one thing. That you'll never put yourself in that kind of danger again."

"As long as you promise me the same thing."

He didn't even hesitate, "Deal."

Despite their exhaustion and injuries, Rose knew that they both needed each other right at that moment. When she kissed him, he tangled his uninjured hand into her hair and kissed her like she was the only thing that could save him.

She moaned and opened her mouth wider. Soon, she was under him, his body arching over hers so as not to crush her. Her heart pounded as he pushed her torn shirt up, and she helped him strip it off her, only breaking the kiss for a second.

"God, I love you," he said as he gazed into her eyes. "I love you more than I can ever say."

"I love you, too." She caressed his jaw, and he nuzzled against her fingers. "You've saved me, Seth. Over and over again."

He kissed her again as they continued to strip out of their clothes. When they were finally, blessedly naked, Rose ran her hands down his body. She felt the bumps of his vertebrae, moving downward until she could grip his muscled ass. His cock jumped between them, and she moved so her legs were parted and he could settle between them.

Seth winced, his forehead creasing, and Rose pushed him to roll onto his back.

"Don't make your arm worse," she chided as she climbed on top of him. "Besides, this lets me have some fun first."

Seth groaned, and then he swore when she licked down

his torso, swirling her tongue around his belly button. His cock was like an iron brand against her skin. She smiled as he swore again when she nipped the tender skin near his pelvis.

He was so beautiful—all warm skin and sleek muscles. His hands were large, his feet equally so, his arms and legs seemingly never-ending. She loved the way his thighs flexed when her hair brushed against them as she moved downward. She loved how his eyes turned glassy with desire as he gazed at her.

She took his cock in her hand, feeling its heat and its weight, and she licked it from the base to the tip. He grew larger in her hand, and she licked a bead of moisture from the tip.

His throat contracted as she dipped down to take him further into her mouth. His hands fisted in the sheets as she loved him that way, almost taking him to the hilt.

Muttering nonsense, he panted, and she could feel him growing close to release. With one last twist of her hand around him, she kissed his belly, his pounding heart.

"You're amazing," he said. "I can't believe you're mine."

"Believe it."

He hefted her breast in his uninjured hand, thumbing her swollen nipple. She tilted her head back as he took one breast into his mouth and then the other. His arm encircled her waist to keep her in place. She squirmed, needing him deep inside of her.

Rose pushed his hand away and took his cock in her hand. Lodging him at her entrance, she slowly sank down on him. They both groaned aloud at the sensation. Shivering, she stayed still, never wanting this to end.

Seth let her go slowly, although she could tell it was killing him. She rode him like she had when they'd first made love, but this time, there was nothing between them.

Rose didn't care. She wanted nothing between them, and if she got pregnant, she would only be the happiest woman in existence.

"I'm close." Seth closed his eyes.

"Not yet." Lifting off him, she told him to sit up. He raised an imperious eyebrow, which just made her laugh.

"When did you get so bossy?" He swore when she faced away from him and sank down onto his cock again in one swift stroke. Seth snaked an arm around her waist, holding her flush against his torso, and he took over the rhythm.

His cock plunged into her as he kissed and licked her neck, her shoulder. Pushing her hair away from her throat, he bit down on the tendon there, making her cry out to the ceiling.

He filled her with endless strokes. Rose could feel her orgasm gathering, and when she began to rub her clit, it descended upon her like a lightning strike. With one last plunge of his cock, Seth brought her to her peak. She screamed, arching and writhing, and it was only his arm around her waist that kept her from collapsing onto the bed.

He thrust once, twice, and then shouted as he came, too. His cock twitched inside her, and she moaned as he filled her with his seed.

The sun was peeking through the blinds when they pushed the covers down to go to sleep. Snuggling beside Seth, Rose yawned.

"I love you," she whispered, tracing his jaw.

He opened one eye to look at her. "Go to sleep." He kissed her on the nose. "And I love you, too, hummingbird. I'll never let you go again."

And Rose knew that he spoke the truth.

EPILOGUE

"Okay, I'm ready." Rose glanced one more time in the mirror, checked her makeup for the thousandth time, and took a deep breath.

She walked into the living room, feeling rather absurdly exposed. Seth's eyes widened.

"Well?" she said, trying not to fidget. "Is it stupid? I'll take it off—"

"No, no. I love it." His grin was swift as he pulled her close and into his lap. "The wings are amazing."

"Really? Do I look like a hummingbird? I thought I might look more like a blue jay—"

"No way. It's perfect. Best Halloween costume ever."

She looked at his costume and rolled her eyes. "You're not even in a costume!"

"Yes, I am." He showed her a sign he'd made that read *Nudist on Strike*. "I'm on strike, babe."

"Oh well, does that mean you're on strike for me? Because that's a damn shame."

He nuzzled her neck. "No way. You can get me naked anytime."

She laughed, and he kissed her, although she eventually pushed him away because she was not going to let him ruin her makeup. She'd gone all out: with blue-green eye makeup and false eyelashes, she'd barely recognized herself when she'd finished. To top it off, she'd glued sequins to the corners of her eyes, although she had a feeling they would be bugging her all evening.

Her costume itself was simple: a shimmery teal slip dress that she'd found at a consignment shop downtown that had screamed hummingbird. She'd bought a pair of fairy wings and added sequins and paint to match her makeup and dress.

Seth glanced down at her feet. "Nice shoes."

"Aren't they amazing?" She'd found some sparkly black stilettos that she knew would kill her feet within an hour, but she didn't care.

The price you pay for beauty—and great Halloween costumes.

When they arrived at Harrison and Sara's house for their Halloween party, they were quickly converged upon by their friends and family.

After the Johnny incident, Rose and Seth's relationship had progressed quickly, and by the end of the summer, Rose had moved in with Seth. She'd teased it was because he had better furniture, but in reality, she hadn't wanted them to be separated—even by a wall. Callie had loved the plush couch in the living room, and despite Rose's best efforts, the end of the couch on the right side had become Callie's spot from then on.

"Oh, I love your costume!" Sara said as she hugged first

Rose, then Seth. She raised an eyebrow at Seth. "Did you forget it's Halloween?" Sara was dressed as a purple grape, her rounded belly only adding to her costume. They were having a boy, news which James had met with almost more excitement than his parents.

Seth grinned and held up his sign. "I'm on strike."

"Men," Sara groused. She took Rose's arm as they headed into the house. "You need to get your man in line," she teased.

Rose looked over her shoulder. "Don't worry. He does pretty much anything I want him to do."

"Good. You can't trust any of these Thornton men to know anything." Sara laughed when Harrison rolled his eyes at her as they approached. "You know it's true."

"Hmm, I'm not answering that." Harrison gave Rose a quick hug, although the wings almost hit him in the face. "You keeping my brother in line?"

"Of course."

Seth had contacted his CO two days before his deadline and told him he wasn't going to take his offer. Sergeant Loyd had been put out, but after Seth had explained his reasoning, Sergeant Loyd had sighed and told Seth that he was an idiot but that he understood.

"You're going to turn into some soccer dad with five kids, aren't you?" Sergeant Loyd had said, albeit good-naturedly.

Seth had laughed. "You never know."

Soon thereafter, Alan had asked Seth to work full-time, and had even mentioned Seth's taking over the business once Alan had retired. With no children and only his wife, Alan had planned on closing when he retired, but Seth would be the perfect man to take it over.

Honored and surprised, Seth had accepted. He and Rose

had celebrated with their own party—mostly in their bed—that night.

It was strange, Rose thought as she chatted with everyone, how things had fallen into place. Her life had been a series of disasters up until now, but it was like Seth had become the anchor she'd needed. Now she had a home, a man she loved, and a future that was bright and exciting. She was going to return to school in January at the local community college to finish her English degree.

After that? The sky was the limit.

Johnny would go on trial within the next few months, although he'd remained in jail because it was, ironically enough, safer for him there than it was in the outside world. His so-called buddies had turned on him when he'd ratted them out, and now they were out for his blood.

Rose was glad that Johnny now got to experience the terror he'd instilled in so many people. It was a small price to pay for what he'd done to her, to Heath, and to countless others.

Both she and Seth had begun to see therapists to talk about their PTSD and nightmares. Although they both still suffered from nightmares, they were happening with less frequency. Having someone to talk to had been liberating, Rose had found. It was one thing for your family and friends to agree that something was terrible; it was another to find that validation in a third party.

"Rose! Your costume is amazing!" Jubilee, wearing a flapper dress and headband, bounced up to Rose. "Did you make the wings?"

"Kind of. I decorated them." Rose had never seen Jubilee wear a dress this short or this kind of makeup—smoky and sensual with a bright red lipstick—and she had to approve. She'd even cut her hair recently into a short, stylish bob, which went with her costume perfectly. Jubilee looked gorgeous.

"How have you been? I feel like it's been ages." Jubilee smiled shyly. "How's my brother?"

"Wonderful. But don't get me started on that subject or you might hear something you don't want to."

Jubilee snorted. "Have you seen my siblings? They have no shame. I went to the bathroom earlier, only to find Caleb kissing Megan and feeling her up in a dark corner." She rolled her eyes. "You guys are a bunch of teenagers."

Rose laughed, mostly because Jubilee was the youngest of them all yet seemed like the oldest in a lot of ways. Jubilee murmured something about getting them both drinks right when Heath strolled up. His costume was a loose sport coat, a sweater, and spectacles.

"Heath, you're not supposed to dress up as yourself," Rose joked.

"I'm Professor Lupin! You know, from Harry Potter?" He pulled out his makeshift wand and acted like he was casting a spell.

"And why do I feel like you remembered that this was a costume party only an hour ago?"

"Not true. It was two hours ago."

They laughed, although Rose couldn't help but notice the strain around her brother's eyes. Ever since the Johnny incident, Heath had been distant, and Rose knew he still blamed himself for what Johnny had done to her. She'd tried to assure him that she didn't blame him, but he'd refused to discuss it.

"You look great," he said quietly. "I'm happy for you."

It was silly, but she felt tears prick her eyes. She touched Heath's arm. "Are you happy? Because I think after everything, we both deserve to be happy."

"Happy enough." His smile was forced. Rose was about to pry into that remark when Jubilee returned bearing drinks.

"Here you go—oh, Heath. Hi. What's your costume supposed to be?"

"Professor Lupin."

Jubilee smiled. "Are you going to turn into a werewolf tonight? It's a full moon, you know."

"Is it? Then you should watch out if I turn wild."

Rose widened her eyes and drank her punch. The sexual tension was rampant between these two, as it had been for months now. Except as far as Rose knew, Heath hadn't asked Jubilee out, and Jubilee was too shy to ask a guy out.

As if realizing what he'd said, Heath muttered something about getting a drink and walked away without another word.

"Hey, there you are. Apparently they're doing a toast or an announcement or something," said Seth. He kissed Rose's cheek. "Hey, Jubi. You look nice."

"Thanks. Looks like you forgot your costume."

"Nah. I got it covered." He showed Jubilee his sign, which resulted in Jubilee rolling her eyes.

Trent and Lizzie arrived then with Bea dressed as a lobster in a giant cooking pot, which meant that Bea became the most popular person there. Even Seth demanded that he get a picture with his niece. Bea yawned and fell asleep in her pot soon thereafter, and Trent carried her around the party for the rest of the evening.

"Ladies and gentlemen, boys and girls, may we have your attention please?" Caleb yelled into the crowd as he stood on an ottoman. "Excellent. Glad everyone could make it tonight."

"Dude, it's not even your party!" Harrison called.

"Unimportant. Megan, can you come up here?"

Megan climbed up beside Caleb, looking pink-cheeked, and Rose had a feeling she knew exactly what they were going to announce.

"Don't worry, Megan said I had permission to do this." Caleb smiled so wide that it was infectious. "Megan and I are happy to announce that we're expecting."

That resulted in a collective shout and applause from the crowd. Seth said into Rose's ear, "My siblings are going to be prolific."

Megan yelled over the noise, "We're due in late May."

"Oh, I'm so excited!" Sara pulled Megan down and the two sisters hugged. "Cousins so close together in age!"

"I know. Perfect timing, right?"

James, dressed as a dragon, told his aunt, "You should have a boy like my mom!"

Megan ruffled his hair. "We'll try our best."

Rose hugged Megan and congratulated her before hugging Caleb.

"So, when are you and Seth getting hitched?" he asked.

She shrugged. "We're not in any hurry."

"Uh-huh. That's what we all say, and then it's marriage, babies, white picket fence..." Caleb's eyes lit up as Megan caught his eye, and Rose knew very well how happy he was with all of those things in his life.

Later into the evening, Rose wandered outside to gaze at the full moon. Seth found her and curled an arm around her waist.

"So many babies, so little time," she said, smiling. "Do you think Megan and Caleb's baby will be a boy or a girl?"

"Huh, well, if those are the only two options…"

She elbowed him.

"A boy. Because Caleb would lose his mind trying to keep the boys away from his daughter."

Rose leaned her head against Seth's shoulder. "I always wanted four kids. I'm not sure why. Maybe because it was only me and Heath, so a big family like yours was appealing."

"Four? Well, then, we better get started soon." He turned her in his arms and kissed her. He smiled down at her, but his gaze was serious. "I want to build a life with you, Rose. Marriage, babies, all of it. I love you."

"Same. I can't wait to give you a daughter and have you freak out trying to keep the boys away from her."

Seth laughed. "Deal."

They laughed and talked for a while longer, talking about the future, when they saw Jubilee come around the corner. It was dark enough that she didn't see them, but she was standing near a house light that illuminated her figure.

"We need to do something about Heath and Jubilee," said Rose. "They're driving me crazy."

"Hummingbird, don't interfere. They'll figure it out."

She sighed. "Men are so stupid. You know when Jubilee got her hair cut, Heath saw her that night and didn't say a word to her about it?"

"So?"

Rose glared at him. "*Men.*"

After Jubilee had turned around, her expression sad, Rose closed her eyes for a moment, only to gasp, "The hair!"

Seth blinked at her. "What?"

"The hair! I was so sure it was hers. But if Johnny didn't have Jubilee in the first place, where did he get it?"

"Wait, what?" Seth looked even more confused.

Rose had told Seth all about Johnny lying to her about having Jubilee when she'd met him at the cabin, but in all the commotion, she hadn't told him about the lock of hair. She'd since forgotten all about it in the craziness of moving and creating their new lives together.

"It looked just like hers, because it was the same color as yours." She touched his dark hair, much shorter than that long strand. "So where did Johnny get it in the first place?"

Seth frowned. "We don't know it was Jubilee's."

"I'm sure it was." Rose's eyes widened when the puzzle pieces started to click. "*Heath!*"

"Now I'm worried you have a fever."

She pinched him, and he yelped a little. "No, Johnny broke into Heath's place. What if he stole it from Heath?"

"Why would your brother have a lock of my sister's hair?"

They both stared at each other: Rose with an eyebrow raised, Seth slowly putting it all together.

Then, Seth just said, "Oh."

"This proves he cares about her. Maybe something has already happened between them. And he acts like I'm crazy anytime I mention it!"

"Probably because you're his sister. And he's into *my* sister." Seth groaned. "My brain hurts. I need a drink now."

Rose didn't mention the lock of hair again, but she knew it had been Jubilee's.

The real question was: why had Heath had it in the first place? She knew her brother wouldn't have sneaked into

Jubilee's place or something creepy like that to acquire it. So, had Jubilee *given* it to him?

"I know you're going to turn this into some mystery," Seth said with a wry smile, "and I know I can't stop you."

"I'm glad you know me so well."

"And I love you anyway."

She gave him a smacking kiss, which resulted in him pinching her ass. "I love you, too," she gasped.

"My princess," he said, and they returned to the house, laughing together.

Jubilee Thornton gazed into the mirror and said to herself, "Stop being such a scaredy-cat." She thrust a finger at her reflection, which she barely recognized. With the short hair, the makeup, and the Halloween costume, she'd felt like a new woman. A sexy, confident woman.

A woman who could get any man she wanted—except that one she did, in fact, want.

Well, she couldn't blame the man in question, because whenever she was around Heath DiMarco, she turned shy and awkward. She said stupid things. Sometimes she managed to flirt, but he never flirted back.

Until tonight. At least, she'd thought he'd flirted with her.

"Stop. Being. A. Scaredy. Cat." She tapped the mirror one last time for good measure.

Jubilee had been scared her whole life. She'd been scared of dying, she'd been scared of doing things alone. She'd been scared of *living*.

She was tired of being scared, and the only way to overcome her fears was to face them.

She was going to ask Heath DiMarco out. On a date.

Her heart fluttered, and she took a deep breath.

Someone knocked on the bathroom door, making her jump. "Hey, are you done yet? Sorry, but I'm about to pee my pants."

Jubilee opened the door to find Abby on the other side, smiling from a little too much alcohol. "Hey, Jubi. How are you? God, I have to pee."

"So you said."

Abby laughed, and Jubilee shut the bathroom door before everyone saw how much Abby had had to drink that night.

Really, if anyone should be drinking, it should be Jubilee.

It was near midnight when she returned to the living room, where most everyone had been hanging out. Megan sat in Caleb's lap, his hand over her belly, both looking like they'd conquered the world. Rose and Seth had disappeared—unsurprisingly—Sara and Harrison were in a corner whispering, and James had fallen asleep on the couch, Bea at the end of the couch, surrounded by rolled-up blankets so she didn't roll off the couch. Mark was looking at his phone, clearly having had enough socializing for the night.

Trent's brother, Ash, and his sister, Thea, were talking with some of Harrison's coworkers, including Jackie, a nurse at Harrison's practice, and Linda, a fellow teacher at Sara's school. There were some people Jubilee didn't know well, others she didn't recognize.

Despite all of the people, Jubilee felt alone. It had been strange, watching all of her siblings find significant others one by one, until only Jubilee was left.

And who would love her? She'd done nothing extraordinary with her life. She didn't have a fiery nature like Megan, or a sweetness like Sara. She wasn't brave like Rose. She was just…herself.

*Poor Jubilee, she's never done anything, has she?*

She'd heard those words many times, sometimes from her own family members. It hurt—because it was true. She hadn't gone to college, she hadn't traveled; she'd only gotten her own place and a job at Megan's bakery two years ago.

*I can't change the past, but I can change the future.*

With that in mind, she went in search of the man she'd had a crush on since she'd met him seven years ago. She'd never had the courage to do anything about it, because she was shy and self-conscious, and Heath was her brothers' friend. He'd always treated her like a little sister.

Jubilee ducked into the kitchen and only found Trent and Lizzie kissing, which made her roll her eyes as she hurried out. She wandered outside, rubbing her arms from the chill. She should've brought a jacket, but it would've ruined her costume.

Her dress swished as she moved, and her heels almost got stuck in the mud from the latest rainstorm. Leaves crunched under her heels, the perennial sound of autumn.

Harrison's house wasn't as large as her parents', but it certainly wasn't a tiny bungalow, either. He had a swimming pool in the back, along with a small garden next to the pool that allowed a measure of privacy.

Jubilee had always wondered if Harrison hadn't installed the garden on purpose for his own rendezvous.

She was about to give up when she heard someone mutter something. Coming around a bend, she found Heath sitting on a bench, his legs outstretched, his arms crossed. He started a little when she approached.

"Sorry, didn't mean to scare you," she said, breathless. The moon had edged him in white light, and it was rather absurd, but it made him seem mysterious. Like a prince from a fairy tale.

*Don't be an idiot*, she admonished herself.

"Jubilee, what are you doing out here? You'll freeze." Standing, he shrugged out of his sport coat and draped it over her shoulders.

She noticed that he didn't linger in touching her. In fact, he seemed to toss the coat onto her instead.

Pulling the coat closer, she inhaled his scent from the fabric. The residual warmth enveloped her, making it seem like he was embracing her.

"Thank you," she murmured. "What are you doing out here? Howling at the moon?"

His lips quirked. "Not exactly, just have a lot on my mind."

"Like what?"

He blinked in surprise before looking away. "Nothing that should matter to you. It's cold out here—let's go inside."

"No." At his confusion, she added, blushing, "No, I mean, we can stay out here. I'm not cold now. Are you cold?"

It took him a long moment to reply. "No, I'm not cold."

*Ask him out. Ask him out. Ask him out.* The words were on the tip of her tongue, waiting to jump into the deep end. She felt her toes curling over the edge of the diving board.

"Heathwillyougooutwithme," she blurted.

"What?"

She took a deep breath. She thanked the darkness for hiding her bright red cheeks. "Heath, will you out with me?"

His stillness sent her hope spiraling down, down, down. He cleared his throat, pushed his fingers through his hair—hair that was the same color as the russet leaves of fall. "Jubilee, I'm flattered—"

She held up a hand. Suddenly, she wasn't nervous: she was irritated. God, when would people treat her like an adult?

"But I'm Harrison's sister. I'm too young. You already have somebody else. I get it."

"No—yes. Kind of." He sighed. "It's complicated."

She didn't know what caused her to do what she did next. Maybe it was insanity, or sheer bravado. Maybe she was just tired of being pathetic and lonely.

Or maybe she wanted to show Heath that he was making a mistake.

Slipping out of his coat, she moved toward him, until only an inch or two stood between them. She heard him catch his breath, and she exulted in that quiet sound. It meant he wasn't as uninterested in her as he'd like her to think.

Jubilee didn't say another word; talking seemed pointless. Her heels gave her extra height so that she wasn't much shorter than Heath now. And before she could think about what she was doing, or the consequences, or that all of her brothers were only yards away, she tangled her fingers in the hair at the nape of his neck and kissed him.

He froze when her mouth touched his. Then, a split second later, he hauled her against him and ravished—positively *ravished*—her mouth until she couldn't catch her breath.

And then, as soon as it had started, it ended.

He was panting, and so was she. Her body sizzled.

"You need to go," he said, his tone harsh.

He wanted her—she knew it. She bit back a smile.

"This is never going to happen." He picked up his coat and flung it over his shoulder. "Don't do that ever again."

Jubilee's initial bravery wilted in the face of his disdain. Perilously near tears, she replied, "Then you shouldn't have enjoyed that kiss as much as you did."

His face was stark in the moonlight. "You're right. I shouldn't have." His tone gentler now, he said, "Go back to the house."

"Fine." She sounded childish, and it frustrated her even more. Turning, her ankle turned on the soft ground, and Heath caught her before she fell.

"I'm fine." She blushed, humiliated. Wrenching her arm away, she stalked away, her dignity in tatters.

She went to the bathroom again and sat on the toilet seat. Forcing the tears back, she pulled herself together. Anger stirred in her belly, and she was rather tempted to smash a vase sitting on a shelf overhead.

"He's a coward," she told her reflection. Reflection Jubilee was flushed, her lipstick smeared, and her hair a mess. She looked like hell.

After she put herself to rights, she pointed at herself one last time. "Don't get mad," she commanded. "Get even."

# ABOUT THE AUTHOR

A coffee addict and cat lover, Iris Morland writes sexy and funny contemporary romances. If she's not reading or writing, she enjoys binging on Netflix shows and cooking something delicious.